VISIONS OF A STARCHILD

VISIONS OF A STARCHILD

Bridgett Chapel

iUniverse, Inc.
New York Lincoln Shanghai

Visions Of A Starchild

iUniverse books may be ordered through booksellers or by contacting:

iUniverse
2021 Pine Lake Road, Suite 100
Lincoln, NE 68512
www.iuniverse.com
1-800-Authors (1-800-288-4677)

ISBN-13: 978-0-595-33124-6 (pbk)
ISBN-13: 978-0-595-84185-1 (cloth)
ISBN-13: 978-0-595-77911-6 (ebk)
ISBN-10: 0-595-33124-6 (pbk)
ISBN-10: 0-595-84185-6 (cloth)
ISBN-10: 0-595-77911-5 (ebk)

Printed in the United States of America

Dedicated to my family, friends and to all Lightworkers, that we may be united to continue our true missions on Planed Earth. Each of us receives our own visions, but it is our choice to carry them out.

This is my story.

To Jimmy,
Thank you
for your support,
It's been great working
with you. Best;
Wishes
July 31, 2006
Bridgt
Chapel
2202

C O N T E N T S

▼

Dreams…. a world of imagination, illusions. The land that exists only in sleep or slumber. To some people dreams are just a succession of images, thoughts, or emotions occurring during sleep. However dreams to some people are more than just a dream. Dreams to these curtain individuals are means of communication. It is a tool for them to reach other dimensions or worlds. These different dimensions could see your future; you're past lives, early childhood experiences, or out of the body episodes. This is true for this one Indian girl. It's not a belief it's an experience.

CHAPTER 1

▼

CHAPEL/STARCHILD

"Be careful." I had no doubt heard my mother say those two simple words perhaps a thousand times during my first four years of my life. Just like millions of other 4-year-olds throughout the United States had done day-after-day. Nothing unusual about that! Nothing mysterious. At least, it shouldn't have been.

But never had those words carried as much concern or subconscious dread than on that fateful summer day in 1954.

We lived in the midst of the heat of New Mexico; in an Aztec Indian family, which somehow defied the laws of physics and became home to a family of nine. My mother, Maria, My father, Lujan, My four brothers: Adrian 17, David 14, Javier 10; Sergio three months, and three sisters, Jessica 12, Eva 8, Alicia 6, and of course, myself—Bridgetta at the age of four.

My father was a mechanic and rented a shop that he managed. He also managed to keep the bills paid and us all fed. Because of this, we enjoyed the basic comfort offered to the average American in the early 1950s. I never noticed that we were just another American Indian survivor. We had a lot less then other families; we always seemed to have more out of life to make our childhood as happy as any. Happier than some, I would latter learn.

Though all our clothes were bought only once a year, my mother always seemed to keep us clean, fed, and get the older kids ready for school on time. Education was my mothers' goal for her children. English was the only language we were allowed to speak. She wanted us to learn as much as we could in the American language and we still kept our belief. My grandmother knew French but she wasn't allowed to teach us. If we wanted to learn another language, it had to be learned at school. My mother had the high-test morals, and always believed to do what was right in the first place. In her dark eyes, she always had a heart and smile of happiness. She had straight black hair as a typical Aztec, but to my dad she was the most beautiful woman he had seen. Her own beauty could not compare with the beauty of her genuine love for my dad even if she was 50 pounds over weight she was happy and so was my dad. He was proud of her and his family witch he had determined to protect like a fist of iron he had.

Like any mother, she would occasionally exaggerate the possibility of danger or injury when it came to her children. We had come to understand and accept it—as any child would. But, on that day, it was different! There was "something" in her voice, her expression, her tone, for a split-second, as she looked down at me with eyes filled with both love and dread, I could feel it. A shiver running up my spine, it was one of the hottest days of the year in the village of New Mexico.

The Morning sun was hot, and bright as we all marched off toward the playground like little adolescent soldiers in search of a new realm to conquer. The concern instilled in me by my mother's two-words directive nothing but a fading memory. "Be careful!"

Though the heat of the day beat down on us like an invisible adversary and fluttering waves of heat rose like transparent weeds reaching up in hopes of finding at least some moisture in the arid air, we marched on. Our minds centered upon the' joy that could be found amidst the rusting, metallic structures wielded and bolted together for the enjoyment of children such as ourselves.

After a few minutes, we stood upon the parched, cracked earth whereupon the metallic structures existed. The monkey bars. The merry-go-round. The swings. The seesaws. And, standing majestically in the middle of it all like some gleaming giant, was the slide. The only "plaything" from that I was forbidden to play on. "Directive" happily enforced by my brother and sister. David and Jessica always made certain I didn't so much as place my small foot on the first metal rung of the long ladder which led to the summit of the slide.

With almost gleeful tones, they would repeatedly warn, "Bridgetta, you know what Mamma said: 'don't get on the slide! You're too little! You could fall and break your arm! Go play on the swings or something, this is for bigger kids!"

With a disappointing felling I would trudge off to the swings and plop down. Kicking my legs back and forth with all my childish anger to make myself go higher and higher. Until, once again with more satisfaction than necessary, David and Jessica would chastise!

"You're swinging too high, Bridgetta, you could fall!"

"Why don't you play on the monkey-bars, Bridgetta?" With frustrated sigh and furrowed brow, I would comply. Only to be warned not to climb so high. I would go to the merry-go-round and be warned not to stand up without holding on while the child-propelled "plaything" whooshed round and round.

Finally, out of desperation and boredom, shuffled over to the seesaws. Which I could not ride without another, of course, so my 10-year-old brother, Javier, was "volunteered" by David to abandon the slide long enough to play with me.

I couldn't help but experience a certain amount of self-satisfaction at seeing my grumbling brother stomp towards the seesaw upon which I sat. His eyes downcast and his hands stuffed in his pockets the way a 10-year-old boy would when confronted with an unpleasant task or chore.

With more force than was necessary, Javier plopped down upon his side of the seesaw and thrust me up. Weighing more than me, all I was capable of doing was dangle on the "plaything" while my 10-year-old brother complained to David," This isn't working She's too small! I might as well be on this thing by myself!"

"Get me down, get me down!" I remember calling out more of a need to aggravate my siblings than any real fear of being in such a seemingly precarious position.

"Javier, let her down!" With a smirk on his pudgy face, my 10-year-old brother joyfully heeded David's directive and gently lowered me to the ground. Climbing off, Javier wasted no time getting back to the slide to resume the playtime ritual of climbing up and swooshing down.

For a few moments, I sat atop the seesaw resting on the ground with tiny arms folded and pouting lip extended in an obvious expression of discontent. Thinking that such would elicit sympathy from David and Jessica so that they would change their minds and let me join the ritual.

I should have known better. It never worked before. Instead, Jessica called out, "Bridgetta, quit sulking! Go over to the sandbox and play!" The sandbox, the very mention of that word conjured up stereotypical images of truly little children playing in the white, sun-bleached grains. Little kids like me! Javier didn't play in it. Jessica didn't play in it. David certainly didn't play in it. But I did. To think, I once found the ides of playing in the sandbox Satisfying. Even exciting! But not anymore, now it was boring. Now it was a reinforcement of the fact that I was only four. I could not play on the slide. That I could not join in the ritual.

Swallowing my pride stood and stomped away. Heading towards the sandbox in a huff, which I had hoped my brothers and sister would notice. If they did, they didn't show it.

They kept playing and laughing. My feelings oblivious disappointment and rejection.

Stepping into it, the warm sand immediately seemed to swallow up my feet. The sand was rising past my shoes and seemingly grasping my ankles. I hated to admit it, but it felt good. Soothing. It almost made me forget that I was mad. Almost. Seating myself began the tedious task associated with all pre-school kids. I made little mounds and plateaus. Traced various images into the white grains. Faces and stick-men and unidentifiable animals, all under the pretense of having "fun". All hopefully aimed at blocking out the laughter heard in the background from David, Jessica and Javier. But no matter how I concentrated on what I was doing, the sound of joy taunted me. Echoing through my subdued disappointment fueling my desire to join them to play on the forbidden structure. It was almost maddening—even for a 4-year-old. I found myself tracing images in the sand, which reflected my innermost feelings. My frustrations. Frowning faces. Fighting stick-men. And one face, which I saw as David, that I promptly used to vent my child-like rage via a straight punch that sent sand flying. Not that I would really want to hit my oldest brother in the face. I loved and respected him. It was just that I was so mad at him for not letting me do what I wanted. It didn't matter that he was merely following directives set forth by our mother. He kept me from the slide. I smoothed out the sand—wiping away the images and the deep hole left by my punch. Then I desperately tried creating more shapes blocking the laughter.

It didn't work!

Finally fed up and overwhelmed with a determination that would resurface through out my life. Also to see me though impossible times, I stood. Fists clinched, jaw set, as I could feel clumps of sand fall from my legs. I automatically brushed away others, which clung to my hand-me-down dress as though they were living creatures that refused to remain in the sandbox. I glanced down as the clumps formed haphazard groupings atop the whiter, smoother sand. I wondered if "they" were upset that I did not take them with me, as I stepped back out onto the cracked earth.

As I walked, I could feel tiny grains of sand between my toes. Trapped within my shoes. Not painful or unduly irritating, just noticeable. However, as I strode towards the slide with arms swinging stiffly at my sides and eyes narrowed in angry determination, the grains were no longer even noticed. Having stalked up to within a couple of feet of the tall, gleaming metal structure, assumed a defiant stance which seemed to imply that I was pursuing some divine "mission".

In hindsight, that description was not far from the truth!

Looking up at David, who was preparing to descend, proclaimed in a no-nonsense voice, I want to play on the slide. And I <u>am</u> going to play on the slide!" I looked up high into the yellow-orange sky ready to change into a desert of red streaks horizon sky.

"Bridgetta, we've already told you: Mamma said you're too little!"

"I don't care what Momma said! I want to slide! I want to play with the light up there! I uh…"

"Bridgetta, listen to David", Jessica angrily interjected. "We're not trying to be mean! We just don't want you to get hurt! If you fell, you could break an arm or a leg or—!"

"I won't fall!" I rudely interrupted while stomping my feet in a fit of childish temper. "All I want to do is slide. Once! Just let me slide once!" The light is flashing right up there. Look! Can you see?" They weren't interested. Just me!

There was a moment of silence. Tense silence, as David and Jessica glared down at me. Almost as if they believed I could be bullied into accepting my mother's orders. It was a tactic they had used before. Successfully. But now I was too determined. The urge merged with my anger I would not be so easily dissuaded again. I would have my way! I would worry about the consequences with my mother later.

For the moment, I just wanted to go up and touch the shimmer light passing back Forth and circling around. After some deliberation, David finally sighed, "Alright". Bridgetta, you can slide! But, if you don't do what I say, we'll take you home to Momma! Deal?"

"Deal!" I squealed excitedly, almost jumping up and down with joy over the prospect of finally getting my wish. The excitement having already chased every last bit of anger from my young mind.

So, with my siblings gathered about to watch with interest and concern, set forth to accomplish what I had longed to do during all these visits to the playground. I reached out and grasped a rung with my hands while placing a foot on the first and pulled myself off the ground.

Then, with increasing excitement, I placed the other foot on the second rung and grasped higher to pull myself further up. One foot then the other. Hands carefully leaving one rung to grasp the next. Up and up and up. Seemingly climbing a metal ladder that reached into the reddish streaked desert sky. My happiness overcoming any worries or fears that might have arisen. At least—until I reached the very top. There I nervously clutched at the curving safety bars on both side and slowly lowered myself into a sitting position. Feeling as though I had just ascended to the top of a multistory structure, instead of a simple slide. Then, with heart racing and breath coming in quick pants, looked down at the ground, which seemed so far below. Down at the faces of my brothers and sister, who were staring up.

Alright, Bridgett David instructed with nerves reassurance in his tone and expression," just reach out and give you a little jerk and slide down. Bring your legs down to catch yourself on the ground so you won't land on your bottom".

I'll be standing there to help you—just in case. O.K.?"I was so scared I forgot about the sparkling light.

Swallowing hard, I nodded and watched as my oldest brother. Did as promised. Moving to take up a ready stance at the end of the long, gleaming incline stretched out before me. I took a deep breath and adjusted my white-knuckled grip on the safety bars. My arms tensed, as I jerked myself forward ever so gently.

"Wheeeee!"

For a split-second, thought the delightful squeal came from someone else. Then, I realized it was I. The brief fears felt now replaced by child-like joy, as I whooshed down the slide at what seemed to me to be a breakneck speed. The air whistling past my airs as it blew my hair back and dried the perspiration on my round face. My stomach tingling as it seemed to momentarily rise then fall. My eyes affixed upon David, he seemed to grow as I rapidly approached his outstretched arms. A smile bursting through the concerned expression, as I reached the end of the metal slide. His hands grasping me lovingly under the arms as my feet plopped into the sand below the slide.

Just then the flashing light swished by my eyes and up again in the sky. I screamed, "I want to go up again! I want to go up again!" "All right, Bridgetta, all right. But remember what I've told you! Take your time climbing the ladder and hold onto the bars before sliding down! Bring your legs down so your feet land on the ground! I'm going to watch you do it once more, and then you'll be on your own. After all, the rest of us want to play, too! You'll have to learn to take turns!" "OK! David, Ok! I want to go again! I want to go again!" I laughed, while skipping back towards the ladder to resume the ritual of little dance of excitement. I got good grip with one hand on the bar and looked to reach for the other side. "Hurry what are you waiting for?" "You take to long!" They all yelled at me. Once again, after finally reaching the top. I jerked myself forward from a seated position to whoosh down towards David's waiting arms. Neither of us feeling as nervous as that first solo slide. Being on top of the slide some how fear would take place and I would forget about the flashing light.

"Very good, Bridgetta", David almost laughed, "keep doing just like that and we'll tell Momma it's alright to start letting you play on the slide with us "Yea!" I cheered merrily, as we all took our respective positions at the ladder. Climbing up and sliding down in single file Just as David, Jessica and Javier had been doing all along. Only now, I was doing it, too!

The ritual was rejoined in joyfulness, as we all took our turns and whooshed down the structure. Up and down. Up and down. The "wheeees" which had come from me those first two times were now coming from all of us. Intermingling with our happy giggles, as we played and the minutes passed with increasing rapidity.

Unfortunately, carefree playing usually led to carelessness. Especially where small children were concerned. It didn't seem fair, but it was nonetheless true. And this day was certainly no exception. On perhaps the hundredth time running from the front of the slide to the ladder to climb again, suddenly sensed a "presence". As though something were nearby. Watching me. Waiting. In fact, glancing off to one side, I could have sworn I saw a transparent form hovering just inches from where I clung halfway between the ground and the top of the slide. David and Jessica having just gone down its incline.

It was odd. Whatever the transparent form was instinctively knew that it was "alive". It knew what it was doing. And it was somehow interested in me. Just me." What're you doing, Bridgetta?"Exclaimed Javier impatiently as he nudged me from below. "Get going! I want to slide!"

Having startled me, I lost my grip on one of the rungs and fell backwards!
"Bridgetta!" Shouted Javier in stunned shock, as I dropped passed him.

Even as I fell, I sensed that the Firelight was following. Maintaining a close proximity. Still waiting. I remember the sudden sensation of sharp, stabbing pain shooting throughout my small body upon impact with the unyielding earth. And I faintly remember the sudden burst of pain in the back of my skull, as my head struck a rock embedded into the ground. Then—everything went black.

All that transpired shortly thereafter, later learned from my brothers and sister.

David and Jessica, having heard Javier's exclamation and my own frightened scream as I fell, rushed to where I lay. David knelt and cautiously lifted me in his arms. Blood quickly coating one forearm where my head dangled as limply as my arms and legs.

"Bridgetta, Bridgetta!" he cried, while trying to control his emotions and keep the tears at bay.

Jessica was in momentary shock and could only stand and stare, while Javier sobbed in a mixture of guilt and grief. "I didn't mean to make her fall, David! I didn't mean to make her fall! I just wanted her to hurry up! I didn't mean to make her fall!"

"I know, Javier, I know!" shouted David while choking back the tears and turning in the general direction of our trailer. "We've got to get her back to Momma! Momma' don't know what to do! Momma will make everything all right!"

In the short time it took for them to cross the distance from the playground to our house it had been tormented by their private thoughts. Javier still believing that my fall was entirely his fault, Feeling as though, if I died, he would be damned for my death. His sobs coming in panicked gasps, as the tears flowed freely and seemingly with no end in sight.

Jessica's shock finally became wails of grief, as she cried all the way to the fixed up house my father repaired for his family. After all I was her only sister, and she always took such joy in helping to clean me up or dress me, almost as if I were <u>her</u> daughter. If something happened to me, she wasn't sure she could endure it.

As for David, he was trying to act like the little man; or at least the way a man was perceived in the late fifties. Holding back the tears until it became a painful lump, which seemed to grow in his throat. And which seemed to slowly tear his heart in half. Though tears welled up in his eyes and his lower lip trembled, he somehow found the strength to resist such an overt expression of sorrow. A sorrow, which intensified with each step he took and with each glance at the limp doll-like form in his arms.

"Momma, Momma, Bridgetta's hurt! Help her, Momma, help her!" Juviair blurted out between sobs, as they entered the fixed up house.

My mother looked up from her ironing and reacted with the expected shock of any parent confronted with their worst nightmare concerning their children.

"Oh, my God! Bridgetta, Bridgetta! My little baby! My little baby! What happened?" She cried, while taking me from David's arms and holding me close to her bosom in a fashion which seemed to suggest she might believe such would breathe consciousness back into my bleeding head.

"We let her play on the slide", David stated in self-guilt, as a single tear managed to escape his control. "She must've lost her grip and fell. She struck her head on a rock. I'm sorry, Momma! I shouldn't have let her!"

Realizing that blaming the children for an accident wasn't going to make me any better, my mother managed to calm herself as the tears formed little oceans of dampness on her cheeks and made the only logical statement that could be made under such circumstances. "I know, I know.

It'll be all right. We'll take her to the hospital. The doctors will make her better. The doctors will save my poor Bridgetta."

We couldn't afford a phone and the nearest neighbor that had one was so far away that it was actually quicker for my mother to take me to the hospital. She would rather do that than wait for an ambulance. So, after wrapping me in a thin blanket to help prevent shock from setting in, my mother carried me out to the old black ford Vicky's car that my dad had rebuilt.

He had pieced together the car with his own hands, and spare parts. He took pride in his work.

After three or four false starts, the engine finally rumbled into life and my mother stomped the accelerator to the floorboard. The car spun out and sped down the winding dirt road, which connected with the nearest highway. Clouds of dust rising, we bounced along in a vehicle, which had had strong shocks and rode more like a racecar. David cradled me in his arms, as my limp form was jostled violently. The wound on the back of my head had slowed its bleeding, but there was still no sign of consciousness or a promise for it. My breathing was all that indicated that life still clung to my small form. The car fishtailed out onto the highway and sped towards the city limits and the hospital wherein my mother hoped I could be helped. All the while praying to her self. Praying that I would be all right. Praying that she could get me to the hospital before it was too late.

Under normal circumstances, my mother was a cautious driver—especially with any of us riding along. But now, she was driving as though she were attempting to come in First Place in a demolition derby. Swerving around cars via the shoulder; blowing the horn incessantly; passing cars and missing oncoming vehicles with a few scant feet to spare.

But, recklessly as it appeared she was driving, I am sure my mother never once placed our lives in danger. She somehow maneuvered along the highway with almost superhuman senses, which prevented an impeding collision from occurring. While racing along the highway, my mother was hurt by the fact that we didn't have a phone at the time. She had to wait to wait until getting me admitted through the emergency room of the hospital, before calling my father on a pay phone in the waiting room to inform him that his youngest daughter had been injured.

She knew that, through my father was one who worked long hours six-days-a-week and even went to work sick, he would not hesitate to leave the shop and rush to the hospital from the other side of the village.

She calls the shop, my oldest brother (age 17) Adrian, Had long black curls falls over his eyes as he answers the phone. "Hello!" "Adrian! Let me speak to your father quickly!" Trying to stay calm, not wanting to show excitement. "Dad, Mom wants you!" He goes sit down on a stool where he plays his guitar while waiting for tourist to show up to buy gasoline at the gas station in the shop where he helps my dad at the shop. The noise generated by mechanics working on various vehicles. My father sliding from under the car bumps his head on the bottom of the car, He doesn't react he keeps on going with grease on his hands grabs a paper towel and reaches for the phone. "Hello!"

Wiping his hands on the grease-stained red rag he kept tucked in his back pocket, my father made his way to the office door. Pushing his personal fears regarding the call out of his forethoughts and hoping for the best.

Respectfully closing the door behind him, my fathers looked at the other employees who where working heavily on a transmission job that are behind schedule

Everyone was in deep concentration. Their work begins 6am until 7pm long hours. With a self-important the phone receiver lying on the edge of the cluttered desk. Picking up the receiver and nervously pressing it to his ear, my father took a deep breath and said, "Hello?"

"Miguel, oh, thanks God! Lujan, there's been a terrible accident!" my mother's voice babbled through sobs. "Bridgetta's fallen from the slide and struck her head! I've brought her to the hospital so the doctors could help her! Oh, Lujan I so frightened".

"Maria, calm down, calm down!" interjected my father with forced control over his fears, as his grip tightened about the black receiver. "How is she? What have the doctors said?"

"I don't know, Lujan the doctors haven't told me anything! Oh, Lujan, I need you so right now! I'm so worried!"

"All right, just calm down. I'll be there as soon as I can. Bye." Hanging up the phone with a little more force than necessary. Lujan glared at his brothers (two of his co-workers) through narrowed eyes of stress and worry and spoke in a commanding tone. "Bridgetta's in the hospital. There was a terrible accident at the playground. We have to leave now Adrian!" With a snap of his fingers. "Grab your machine let's ride." Adrian jumped on his low ride hardly Davidson. And my dad and his brothers jumped on their hogs (Harley Davison). Rumbling vibrations caused dust to be all over the highway on route 66.

A half-hour later the silence in the waiting room was broken, you could hear the rumbling vibrations coming from miles away. My mom knew my dad was near by. She got up from the chair and met him at the emergency entrance. He comforts my mother with an embrace. Then hastily strode down the hallway in search of my brothers and sisters. His stomach muscles tensing so much he felt as though he might throw up and his temples pounding from the repressed fears and grief, my father stopped short of where his children were sitting. Adrian appears washout with grease and dust on his face right behind his dad.

"Lujan!" Exclaimed my mother in simultaneous relief and sorrow. She rushed to embrace him she buried her face into his soiled shirt.

"Lujan, Lujan! What are we going to do?"

Fearing the worst, my father swallowed hard and asked," What have you learned? What have the doctors said?"

"Nothing!" replied my mother while pulling her tear-stained face from his chest and looking up through red-rimmed eyes. "They're still with her!" Feeling a bit relieved, my father forced a reassuring smile to his grease-smeared, sweat-coated face and said," I'm sure everything's going to be all right, Maria. We just have to wait. They'll tell us something soon. Bridgetta will be fine."

Though my father didn't wholly believe his own words, he knew it was necessary to momentarily diminish my mother's anguish, to put aside her most horrid concerns and fears. Though, truthfully, he felt those same fears. For the fact that the doctors had still not emerged to inform them of my condition was perceived as a portent of doom. No news was good news—except in the Emergency Room of a hospital.

As the minutes slowly passed, my mother sat and rocked back and forth while mouthing silent prayers. Jessica continued to sob, as she imagined life without her baby sister. Javier fought back the tears, while mentally blaming himself for what had happened. David, on the other hand, continued to assume the stoic stature of a young man in control of his sorrow especially in the presence of our father. Speaking of whom, he paced the small confines of the waiting room His worries becoming intense, as he watched the time pass and still heard nothing from the doctors.

Finally, my father stormed up to the nurse's desk and glared down at the aging woman-in-white seated behind with her two-neat stacks of paper." I want to see a God-damn doctor right now!"

She startled a moment then tried to calm my dad down. She deals with this type of situation all the time. "Sir, I am very sorry I wish I could help you but there isn't anything I can do. As soon as I hear any kind of progress I'll let you know. Please go to your children, they need to be with you at this time. My father was a patient man, but sometimes when it comes to his children, he wants to do the best that he can to protect them all.

Time passed by very slowly. My father Said, in a soft voice. "Children! Let's all gather together and say a prayer. The creator will hear us he will do what is best maybe he will bring her back to us and make her well again". They gather in a circle and begin to pray. Shortly after the prayer. The doctor entered the waiting room with the message everyone waited to hear. Your daughter is in a coma.", the solemn-faced doctor somberly sighed with hands stuffed nervously into the pockets of his stainless white smock.

The words struck my family numb, as the doctor continued in an almost apologetic tone. Your daughter has sustained a very serious injury to the back of her head. It caused a slight swelling of the brain, which we have managed to alleviate, but which has left her in a comatose state. We can keep her alive temporary. If the change of her swelling does not go down we may lose her. We cannot predict nor guarantee when consciousness might return. If she regains consciousness she could possibly be a vegetable. It would be a miracle that she would be normal again. She has damage to her memory bank. I am very sorry there is nothing we can do but wait. As my mother began crying uncontrollably and my brothers and sisters experienced similar shock, my father placed a firm arm about her and looked directly into the doctor's eyes in a no-nonsense expression.

"We want to see her. Can we see her?" My father asked, as he wiped a couple of tears escaped from his eyes.

"Yes, but just for a short time?" The doctor replied.

The sight of me lying so still in the midst of a huge hospital bed with tubes and wires attached like some tiny machine being overhauled caused my mother to break down into uncontrollable tears again. Even my father found it difficult to contain the tears, as he turned his moist eyes up to stare at the fluorescent lighting in an attempt to maintain control. It had to be the most difficult thing he had ever done. It wasn't that my father didn't feel the same love for David, Jessica or Javier, it was just that I was his little blond curly headed baby girl. She didn't look like the other children that had dark hair. I guess he sensed that too. Something-special existed within me. My mother could not control her grief and turned away to hide the new deluge of tears, which now assaulted her.

Javier, who is usually has a dark-complexion, was now as white as the sheets upon which I'd been placed. He stared down in a wide-eyed horror at what he still believed he had caused. David, poor David. He tried to remain strong, but he finally surrendered to his sorrow. He buried his face in his hands in a vain attempt to muffle his sobs.

Because he had been placed "in charge" of us whenever we went to the playground, he felt personally responsible for my accident. How could I tell him that it was all-unavoidable?

The doctor, who had accompanied my family into my room, noticed the extreme grief etched into their faces and wisely cleared his throat and said,"I"11 leave you alone with her for a few minutes."

After the door closed, my mother managed to pull the lone chair next to my bed and gently squeezed my limp hand in hers. It was as though she were trying to once again revive me by forcing some of <u>her</u> consciousness into me. Her sobs subsided for a moment, as she stared at my face through puffy, bloodshot eyes. "My little Bridgetta, I don't know if you can hear me but, I want you to know how much I love you. How much we all love you. Please, don't leave us, my special baby. Please—don't die. Our lives would lose meaning without you. You made a happy family even more so. I can understand why God would want someone as beautiful and special as you to be one of his angels, but we still need you here. Come back, Bridgetta. Come back."

My mother began crying again; covering her face with her free hand, while still clutching at mine. My father placed a firm, reassuring hand on her shoulder and squeezed with gentle love. Giving her the silent support she obviously needed at that point.

Finally, my mother stared through misty veils of grief at my small face closed, unmoving eyes. "I wonder—what it is you are seeing in your death-like sleep, Bridgetta", she whispered so no one but she and I could hear. If I <u>could</u> hear her.

CHAPTER 2

▼

THE GUARDIAN & THE
CITY OF LIGHTS

I found myself in a dark place. I was a an embryo fetal position. As I wanted to stand, my arms lifted up first. I looked at my arms. I was not a little girl anymore I was something else. I notice light was coming from inside me; there was no sun. I was butterscotch with shimmer, as golden sparkles within me.

As I rose to stand, I looked up in front of me stood a father image. He had held out his arms and his wings under his arm just like me! Somehow he entered words into my mind as if I belonged to him. Telepathic, he said; Jump! Fly! Quickly! You can fly! Your wings use them! Feel your feet! Kick! Jump! Fly! Quickly! (Like a father coaching during labor for a mother). I felt the sand between my toes. I noticed I was standing at the top of a cliff made of moist sand drying by the light as I became brighter. The sand was rapidly falling away from my feet making a smaller area to kick from. Like sand in an hourglass of time.

I bent my knees and spread my arms. I took control of my wings and began to fly. I followed my father image as we flew into darkness. I had to fly faster and faster to keep up with him. The faster I would fly the brighter I became. I felt very happy and excited. Flying hard to keep up but yet I was laughing. (Like a child clapping her hands when she's excited at Christmas time). It felt like we were flying for a long time but a short distance. Up ahead I could see the brightest lights. There were others just like us. We entered his big dome of lighted cliffs. I watched him land at the top of the big mountain filled with cliffs.

I landed right at the edge next to my father image; suddenly darkness began to surround me I turned to my father image confused. Then I heard my name called, "Bridgetta, wait!" I began to remembering....I'm not the girl I used to be anymore. He looked into my eyes. Tears of sadness flooded our eyes. "No! No!" He yelled with all his might. I began falling into darkness. He reached to grab me with his powerful wings but my hair was like corn silk and slipped between his fingers. It felt like His wings swished through the universe with great speed and power.

I came out of the coma in a hospital. I saw my father, my mother, my brothers, and my sisters. My sister whispered in my ear, (trying not to break the silence in the room) "I thought you were going to die." I knew it was the prayer that had brought me back. I felt very disappointed I didn't want to be this little girl. I wanted to go back. I cried in silence. I didn't let anyone know what I went through. I didn't talk to anyone. I was more confused then ever. How could anyone ever understand? Everyone left the hospital so I could get some rest.

The moon was shinning bright through my window I stared at it like in a trans until I fell a sleep. I felt my spirit leave my body lifted very high leaving going up so high above the stars and into darkness with out the knowledge of fear. I was back on the mountain top with my father image I guess he did catch me after all. I was happy and excited to be back. My father wrapped his wings around me and telepathic said: "You found your way back to me. Your here with me now but you can go back and return at any time. Your a very special one."

I no longer felt the same love for my dad. It was different. I felt like he was my guardian, a teporary father until my death. I just realized I had a stronger love for my father up beyond the stars in another dimension. My mom, my three brothers and three sisters entered my room trying to be quiet, yet still making noises as families always do. My mom came to my bedside and my oldest sister opened the window in front of my bed. You can see the room across the hall! My mother said: Look! There is a little girl in that room. Her name is Bridgetta too! She is the same age you are! We have been visiting with her. I could see her waving her hand to us and we waved back. I was still in a state of shock. I didn't want to talk. My mother looked at me and said, "She is going to die. She has leukemia. They don't know how long she has to live."

Later they brought her to my room in a wheelchair. She had a big smile on her face. "Hi, my name is just like yours! We are the same age too!" I just looked with a very short word. "Hi" I said. But all I could do is think. Think about how nice it would be to go where she was going. I didn't talk much at all just looked. They soon took here back to her room. It wasn't long till everyone went home. I stayed in my room in silence. I couldn't tell anyone what had happened.

When I slept, I would return. It was as real as it seemed when I was awake. I felt separated from my body and not just a dream. I tried to think of it as a dream but to me, it was real and I didn't want anyone to know about it. How could they? They couldn't!

As the sun entered my window that next morning so did my family with the sad news, the little girl had died in her sleep last night. The angel of death was there. I knew she would go and fly as I did but I knew she would never return like I did. Yet I don't see her in my dimension. Maybe I will one night who knows maybe, after my death! I didn't want to ever wake up. I didn't want to be here. I will always be waiting for the right time to come for me.

My brothers and sisters kept me busy throughout my life, but I still kept my secret fantasy. I have to go through this alone for the rest of my life.

I was getting use to the out of body experience it was becoming part of my life

I was adapting it like a natural thing for me. I laid my head on my pillow and drifted away. I felt my spirit rise above my bed leaving my body below without a question of thought.

Through the stars and up into darkness and again there I was. With no hesitation or thoughtful Pause, the entity answered athoritately, "Here is—a realm beyond the physical existence of your world! Your Universe! And I—I am your Guardian! As your father! Like your protector! Your Guardian Angel of Death! But not an ending or beginning". The glittering Guardian replied mysteriously. "I Have been watching and waiting since your physical birth, Special One!"

"Why do you call me—Special One?"

There was an eerie silence, as though the Guardian were considering whether or not I was capable of comprehending what it was about to state.

"Once in a thousand human generations, a Special One is incarnated I Filled with all the metaphysical properties and potential power to do what countless others have done since the Dawn of Thought! Battle the Ultimate Evil that periodically threatens humanity throughout Man's history! Not famous leaders or scientific geniuses—but people with normal lives and common vocations! But, nonetheless, Special Ones without whom Mankind would have long since become extinct! Food for the ravenous appetite of the Ultimate Evil!"

Not fully understanding, I changed the subject and asked," How did I get here? The last thing I remember was falling from the slide! Then at night I return to you! I don't have my wings anymore? Why?"

"As you had already perceived, Special One, There is no need for them, you can precede with out them. I hovered nearby! I had to wait for the precise moment before the Merging!"

"Merging?" puzzled. "Allow me to show you/through <u>my</u> perspective, those last moments I commented the voice, as a part of the Guardian's fluid form reached out and made contact with my essence.

Suddenly, I was seeing the accident. But not through my eyes! Rather it was from the Guardian's point-of-view. It was an odd view. The alternating colors partially silhouetted forms. But I could perceive enough to know that it was <u>me</u> I was seeing. Just as I lost my grip and fell. The Guardian rapidly following me all the way down—staying just inches away! I saw myself strike the ground. My head striking the rock, and the blood flowing down my eyes.

"I don't want to see any more!" my voice exclaimed fearfully, as the disturbingly vivid images halted. The Guardian's "touch" retracting; as it's thunderous voice took on a soothing quality.

"Do not fear Special One. You are not dead! At least, not in the permanent sense humans come to associate with that concept! You shall return to your family Special One. Altough you must first meet the chanllenge of the Ultimate Evil!"

"Why can't <u>you</u> do it?" I asked logically.

"Because the Evil is only vulnerable to one who has roots with the living? One who is alive! One of the few who is Special!"

As I listened to the Guardian's strange statements, I noticed the curious colors shading the Infinity in which we floated began to shift. Giving the impression of movement. As though we were riding in the back of a car and watching the scenery speed by and thinking for a moment, that it was the scenery that was moving. When really it was us.

Faster and faster until the colors blurred into one multi-hued shade have defied description. Strangely, there was no sensation of movement of velocity. Yet, it was obvious that we were beginning to travel very fast.

"Where was I going?"

"You shall see very soon, Special One!" I came the reverberating reply, as the colors suddenly vanished and we were swallowed up by a terrifying blackness. A void as endless as the Infinity from whence we started! I was scared! But I knew it wasn't my choice.

"Do not be frightened, Special One! I am with you! I am your Guardian, remember? I shall not let anything happen to you during this journey—to the City of Lights!" I didn't even want to ask what the Guardian meant that!

In what probably seemed like hours, but which was only seconds. A glowing orb in the distance finally disrupted the monotony of the void. Too far away to make out any characteristics, all I could perceive was that we were approaching at an incredible velocity. Probably at or beyond the speed-of-light constant!

Of course, that would mean the glowing orb of white, pulsating light was tens-of-millions of miles away! But, at our current speed, the Guardian and I would reach it within 30 or 40 seconds!

I didn't have to ask the Guardian if the orb was the City of Lights to which he had referred earlier. What else could it be?

One thing was certain: The City of Lights would have to be incredibly huge to be so visible at such a distance! At least as large as Earth's sun!

As I watched the methodical pulsations within the glowing orb, which growled steadily before us, I became almost mesmerized by it. I started to imagine that the orb was some sort of Cosmic Egg and that "something" living inside it was attempting to "hatch". Could I be witnessing the next Big Bang that would create a new Universe after ours died? Or was it the beginning of our own in some dim past? I had no way of knowing or guessing, but we were now less than a few million miles away! And closing fast!

It was then that I noticed a strange shape interconnected to the bottom of the egg-shaped orb of throbbing brilliance. It was another structure of energy, but it was shaped like a pyramid. Such as could be seen in the deserts of Egypt or the jungles of South America! Very dimly illuminated, but definitely there!

At a distance of a few hundred thousand miles, the orb literally filled my view and I noticed that the pulsations within that created by the constant movement of trillions of smaller points of light in a non-methodical fashion.

"Special One—welcome to the City of Lights!" Suddenly, we burst through the "membrane" of energy, which encased the solar-system-sized orb and soared into the midst of the City of Lights!

"Wow!!" Not only was such an exclamation of awe inadequate in connection with such an incredible sight, it should have been embarrassing. Considering the millennia-old entity, which accompanied me and acted as my guide. Still—it did sum up my feelings at that moment better than any other words!

The City of Lights seemed boundless. But I was certain it was not. At least not in the sense that the multi-colored Infinity and the black void were without end. The best way to describe the seemingly improbable city before me was that it was made up of multiple levels of glowing, multi-hued "structures" of energy. Resembling, for lack of a better comparison," buildings" of energy apparently suspended in mid-air and stretching from one unseen "horizon" to the other! Energy constructs totally devoid of such physical trappings as windows or doors and rising higher than any glass-and-steel structure on Earth! And the trillions of energy-points seen from outside the orb as swirling "fireflies" were, I now perceived, disembodied entities such as myself! Souls! Enough to account for every human to have ever walked the Earth since the Dawn of Consciousness!

They moved about effortlessly and with a sense of Ultimate Freedom unlike anything imaginable to their flesh-and-blood counterparts. Moving through various levels of numerous "buildings" with an obvious purpose.

"Is this—Heaven?" I asked with an awed tone while attempting to take it all in.

After a prolonged pause, the Guardian thoughtfully replied, "That <u>is</u> one of the names humanity has given for this Realm! However, the most accurate and more-easily comprehended is simply the City of Lights! It is where, as you have already deduced, any Essence departing your physical plane on Earth comes to spend their Eternity! Unless they choose to reincarnate! Unlike your entry into the City of Lights, most are thrust through what might be scientifically called a Trans-Dimensional Tunnel that carries them swiftly and directly here! A bit quicker than the route <u>we</u> took, Special One!"

Though I clung to every word issued from the Guardian, my visual attention was centered upon the myriad Souls flitting about the vast expanse of the City. I soon sensed that some belonged to deceased relatives of mine. Some I knew well. Some I didn't. Grandparents, great-grandparents, cousins they were all there—along with essences belonging to once-great men of history or science!

Curiously, they were aware of me. Transmitting great respect for me. As though I truly were the Special One that the Guardian claimed me to be.
    Which brought a quite logical question to mind!

"Where are the other Special Ones, Guardian? Why don't I sense them?"

"They are in—other Realms <u>within</u> the City of Lights, Special One!" answered the Guardian with a tone of great respect for them. For me? "They are as apart from the other entities as they are with them! Come! We must go to the very heart of the City!"

Slowly, we began soaring towards the middle of it all. The ease and grace of eagles riding thermal updrafts in the clear blue skies. I found myself, quite naturally, wondering about the purpose of the "buildings" of different colored energies surrounding us and into which the Souls streaked.

As if perceiving the question before expressed, the Guardian explained, "Through the many metaphysical levels of these constructs, these entities may rest, remember and investigate any aspect of Time and Space desired! They may communicate with loved ones left behind, if such is their wish! They may guide or inspire those who meant most to them in their physical lives! There is no 'boredom' or 'complacency' within these structures of solidified cosmic energy, Special One. Their eternity is filled with fulfilling pursuits which defies description!"

Some how I understood. Even though I was the essence of a four-year-old child who hadn't begun kindergarten. It made me happy for all these trillions of Souls which had left their physical existences far behind. As we neared a bright-white "building" in the precise center, I could feel the pervading peace and tranquility that touched each and every entity. The Ultimate Peace and Supreme Happiness for which Mankind had searched all his collective life! Ironically, found only after Life is but an ethereal "memory".

The stories told by parents and grandparents about the Hereafter were, for the most part, true! I was glad."Prepare yourself, Special One", the Guardian instructed with a tone of utter respect," we are about to enter the metaphysical plane of He-Who-Creates!"

"God?" I pondered with a hint of apprehension at meeting the Supreme Being. But the Guardian did not answer. Instead, we were instantly enveloped by a brilliance, which would have agonized my human eyes. But which only awed me in my no corporeal state. Awe beyond any other!

I immediately sensed that we had just penetrated yet another metaphysical "layer" of this multi-leveled Realm and were almost literally at the heart of the All!

I suddenly sensed the presence of an entity of incredible power and Ultimate Knowledge! An entity that emitted an aura of Total Peace and Calm that exceeded what I'd sensed earlier! Then I saw a form! A gently shifting shape that towered over the Guardian and me! Filled with a brilliance that would dwarf the radiance of a noonday sun! Was I in the presence of God? I was not sure. But, whoever this bright-white essence was— He was without equal in the City of Lights!

There were no words. No telepathic contact. No images. He Who-Creates was communicating with me on a level that had no label! In a matter of moments, I knew all I needed to know! About Why I was there. Why I was a Special One. Why Special One's were necessary. And the basic nature of my first encounter with the Ultimate Evil!

I also came to know that, even after returning to my body and my physical life, I would be "called upon" to channel my entity into other Realms wherein the Evil fed and had to be "challenged"! I knew—and I felt no fear. No doubts. No reluctance.

But then, in the "heart" of the City of Lights in the very presence of the Supreme Entity, how could I feel such useless emotions?

CHAPTER 3

▼

THE JUNGLE OF EVIL

"Why are we going to that building, Guardian?" I asked with a little bit of worry on my face. As we found ourselves streaking towards the middle of the reddish-glowing energy construct situated some distance from the "heart" of the City of Lights. Though my communion with the Supreme Being answered the overall question regarding why I was there and what I had to do, it did not answer such trivial details as this. I had to rely upon my Guardian for this one.

"Through there, Special One, you shall enter one of a multitude of extra dimensional levels wherein the Ultimate Evil is making yet another attempt to help lead humanity to obliteration!" the Guardian replied with a hint of concern. Then, as we were a few feet from the glowing, red "surface" of the structure, he added one last bit of instruction. "From here, you must go alone, Special One! I am not allowed to enter any of the Realms of Evil! But always remember: Just as it is when you are in your physical form on Earth, so is it true during such 'challenges' that I am always watching over you! A part of my own strength shall constantly be channeled into your essence! The greater the threat you face, the more strength shall be channeled! Such is my function, Special One! But it is <u>you</u> who shall actually do battle with the Ultimate Evil! It shall be <u>you</u> who defeats it!"

With that being said, and the Guardian halting his momentum, I gathered all the courage imparted to me by the Supreme Being. Then I exerted a powerful thrust that sent me hu heading towards the building.

An explosive burst of bright red was followed by a deep blackness that in turn, dissipated to permit me to see my surroundings. For a moment I almost wished I could not.

Though there was very little illumination, could see well enough to make out certain details. The first of which shocked me. I was apparently backed in my true body! Wearing a long, white gown of some unknown material with no shoes on my feet and sat on a highly uncomfortable bench! I instinctively knew that the "body" was not flesh-and-bone, but rather a shell of energy that encased my essence and merely took on the appearance of my physical form.

Then, I noticed that I was definitely not alone. There were many thousands of humans sitting on the other benches like mine that stretched for perhaps a mile along the length of the interior of what appeared to be some sort of Ark! An incredibly huge one! A mile or more in length; about 200 feet in width; a thousand feet high. At least, such were the dimensions of the hold in which I found myself with these others. No doubt the vessel was, in truth, much wider and taller than this!

The people gathered in the Ark's hold were of all spirits gather no color no race, not even religion was recognized. It was a negative energy field. I had a mission to accomplish without choice. I questioned myself, why do I have to save those evil spirits? Why are they getting a second chance? Some even appeared to be from different historical time-periods!

There were only two things they all had in common: They, too, were garbed only in white gowns. And they were all adults! Other than me, there was not a single child amongst them! I found that curious, but recalled how my mother had always told us that children always went to Heaven when they died. Never to Hell!

Of course, I didn't know for certain that this place was part of Hell. Anymore than I knew for certain that the City of Lights was Heaven. All I did know was that this Ark and whatever their destinations were at the opposite end of the spectrum from the City of Lights!

This was substantiated by the fact that I sensed nothing but fear and anxiety about me. Whereas in the City of Lights! I felt only peace, happiness and calm. Besides, the expressions on the sea of faces about me all bore an unspoken terror for which all seemed certain awaited them. Somehow! I knew it, too!

The Ark was apparently moving, though there were no such sensations to confirm that suspicion. Touching the colorless surfaces of the bench and the curving wall, I shivered at the thought of how it seemed as cold as a tombstone in the dead of winter. I also found it strange that the minimal lighting within the huge hold seemed to have no logical source. It was just there! That dispelled any doubts that the Ark existed in my own physical dimension of Reality. For, in that plane of existence, the laws of physics would dictate that there would have to be a source!

Which led me to suspect that these other humans were not of true flesh-and-blood, but rather disembodied essences encased in shells resembling their bodies. Just like me. I assumed that the no corporeal shells were meant to prevent their essences from doing what should seem "natural" after physical death. Passing through the no doubt dense walls and soaring away. whatever form the Evil utilized in this Realm, it was necessary to create the illusion of solidity that would be so fresh in the memories of these poor Souls! I had a distinct advantage over all gathered within the belly of this massive vessel. I knew! Where I was—why I was there—and the Ultimate Evil to which the Ark traveled! This knowledge, along with the inner strength channeled into me from my Guardian, gave me an edge. Terror could not place me in its oppressive grasp!

Still, my commune with the Supreme Being could not prepare me for the tremendous sorrow I felt for these Lost Souls. Consumed with a fear for which they had no control. Agonized by the realization that, very soon, they would have to disembark the massive Ark. Not only that but, face an Ultimate Eviil for which they had not been fully prepared! They were going to meet their God of destruction. (Satan) The Ultimate Evil!

I imagined that such horrified, confused expressions were common amongst the faces of Jews being loaded into boxcars like cattle and sent to Nazi concentration camps for inevitable torment and death. I sensed that the Nazis, and that entire terrible period of Man's history, was an example of how close the Ultimate Evil must have come to actually fulfilling its dark Destiny! The stranglehold it must have to create such a reality in which otherwise normal men became such mass murderers must have been great!

Whoever the Special One was in the mid-to-late 1930, they must have had one hell of a "challenge"! I found myself hoping that I could be as successful. On a subliminal level! I knew I would, thanks to my commune with the Supreme Being and my continual tie with the Guardian. But I still couldn't help but at least hope that success was achieved. I still couldn't help but feel a little nervous. After all, I was only the essence of a 4-year-old girl!

I couldn't help but think of how this confrontation I was about to have with the Ultimate Evil would make the biblical battle between David and Goliath seem evenly matched by comparison!

Suddenly, the Ark lurched. As though it were slowing. Such could only mean that we were nearing our hellish destination. The others became even more fearful. Their eyes wide in terrified anticipation. If they had actually been in their physical bodies, I imagined they would all be perspiring profusely at this point. Many would be crying like children. A few probably would even lose control of certain bodily functions!

In these fake forms, only their facial expressions could denote the terror felt within.

Another lurch. Now it was obvious the Ark had been moving and was slowing. You could actually feel it. The fear shared by the many thousands within the vessel's hold now gave rise to unintelligible mumbles that reminded me of the buzzing I once heard within a hornet's nest in a tree not far from our trailer. I half-expected panic to erupt and cause the people to crush one another in a senseless stampede. Somehow! I knew it wouldn't come to that.

In the tense moments before the final lurch of the Ark that would signal it had stopped. I couldn't help but wonder what these people could have done that was so terrible. It insured them a place on this vessel. What could they have done in their lives that, upon their death, they would been gone to the potential horror that awaited them outside? None had the appearance of murderers, child abusers or war criminals. In fact, all of them I could see in the limited illumination seemed as normal and

God-fearing as my own parents! Perhaps it was their own doubts in their lives and an uncaring attitude about the world about them, which placed them here. Perhaps it was that one vagrant they shunned on some city street when all he asked for was enough to buy something to eat. Perhaps it was all some sort of Cosmic Mistake! Whatever the reasons, it was obvious by my presence that I was supposed to save as many of them as possible. I simply had to trust in the Supreme Being and my Guardian—and accept the "challenge" which laid before me!

The Ark came to a sudden halt that nearly tossed us from our benches, as the worried mumbles rose to a horror-stricken roar! Then there was an almost electrical hum, which assumed a thunderous volume and a rumbling that tickled the souls of my feet and coursed throughout the flooring of the mile-long hold! At the far end, I could see the lower half of the vessel's bow actually opening! The huge ramp-door slowly lowering and the brilliant daylight outside flooding the interior through the rapidly parting seams!

We had arrived! As though responding to some unspoken command, everyone stood and took their places in a double-line down the middle of the hold. I stood as well in order to proceed with my "mission". In the moments it took for those with whom I stood to commence their slow march towards the lowering ramp-door, I peeped past the taller adults and saw the tops of trees which suggested a jungle area. A conclusion which was promptly confirmed by the appropriate animal sounds which filtered in above the thunderous hum and frightened mumbling!

The stale air inside the Ark was suddenly assaulted by the steamy humidity of the jungle, as the ramp-door apparently halted its deafening function and the first of the thousands made their reluctant descent into the unknown. Almost immediately, there were unearthly roars, which literally caused the massive Ark to tremble followed by horrified shrieks from those having disembarked seconds before! It was the Ultimate Evil! Curiously, in the face of the obvious torment being encountered by those leaving the Ark, no one inside halted their obedient march forward. None gave in to the panic that no doubt dwelt within them and attempted to stay inside the hold!

Instead, with pale expressions of dread, they continued towards the gaping exit and the ramp-door leading down to an unspeakable "thing" which continually bellowed its monstrous roars! And the shrieks of agonized realization echoing into the distance.

Much sooner than desired, the section of Lost Souls in which I "obediently" marched came to the edge of the lowered ramp-door and I looked out. As if the steamy jungle and reddish sun burning through the grayish haze wasn't enough to send shivers up the back, I saw the source of the monstrous roars and the cause of the agonized shrieks! A gigantic reptilian Beast standing nearly 200 feet taller than the trees!

It seemed a sick combination of reptilian creatures with proportions skin to the dinosaurs of pre-human history on Earth! Fire from his eyes that denoted no emotion or mercy! A full definition of Anger! A series of horns protruding up through the top of its head and descending down the back of the neck! A short snout filled with razor-sharp fangs measuring at least 10 feet in length! Forked tongue, similar to snakes—only thousands of times larger! Heavily muscled arms akin to a human body-builder! Massive six-fingered webbed hands with long, sharp talons which it used in steam shovel fashion to scoop up Lost Souls and "pour" them into its gaping maw! Swallowing them whole! Their muffled shrieks heard from deep within—in some other hellish Realm for which I did not wish to even hazard a guess!

Its massive feet, half-buried in the dense underbrush, had three clawed toes on the front and one "spur" on the heel! And there was a long, alligator-like tail swishing back and forth with devilish delight, as the shrieks of horror melded with its thunderous roars! If I had not been instilled with courage by the Supreme Being! I would have been terrified! As it was, I only felt bewilderment over the way the Lost Souls continued walking down the ramp-door towards their obvious fate! It was as though they were trapped within the Beast's unseen influence! Perhaps they had been during their physical lives, as well. Such might very well explain <u>why</u> they were "damned" to this Realm of Evil!

Slowly, I began down the ramp-door. Thus far, the Beast didn't seem to sense my presence. So far—I still had the edge in this situation. But, I wondered, for how long?

The closer I got to the towering creature, the less humid heat I felt from the surrounding jungle. It was as though I were descending into the depths of a chilled crypt! Shivers crept up my back, as I decided to make my move. Being the smallest I guess I wasn't as noticeable, or as important.

I leapt from the side of the ramp-door to land, cat-like, on the jungle floor several hundred feet below! The defiantly individual move instantly caught everyone's attention! Including the Beast!

As I turned, couldn't help but notice the Ark that hovered just above the tree line. As I suspected, the true dimensions of the strange vessel was much larger than those of the hold. Whatever the material was constructed from, it was most certainly not anything known to Man. If I didn't know better! I would have sworn it was a starship from some other world!

But my attention was quickly diverted back to the monstrosity towering over me, as its shadow fell across my tiny form and its snout snarled in disapproval of my action. Then, it obviously perceived what I was and why I was there, because my mind was suddenly assaulted by a telepathically delivered voice that growled with an ageless Evil.

"So, another Starchild has come to challenge me! Good! It has been far too long since the last one and I do grow so bored with consuming these spineless spirits! Their torment can only satisfy me for so many decades, you know!"

Suddenly, as he exhaled, the stench of his foul breath assaulted me! It was like standing next to a million rotting corpses if I had been in my true physical body, I would've no doubt vomited! As it was, I only felt the nausea!

Delving into my courage, as it became obvious that the Lost Souls could not "hear" the telepathic voice of the creature, I responded in kind!

"You have been defeated before by other Star-children, Evil One, and you shall be defeated again! You shall never reign over humanity! You shall never destroy my kind!"

Brave words from such a small spirit! chuckled the Beast malevolently, as it leaned closer.

Sensing what it was about to do and noting that its attention was no longer centered upon the Lost Souls, I took a deep breath and shouted, "Run!!"

For perhaps the first time in a dozen decades, these seemingly mindless Souls shook off the Beast's "spell" and fled for the safety of the surrounding jungle! Needless to say, the monstrous embodiment of Evil was not "pleased"!

It glanced at the fleeing and sceaming spirts. Then glared back down at me with those fire burning reptile eyes and snarled, "You shall suffer for this, insolent Starchild!"

As it lifted one of its massive feet to crush me, I turned and ran with all the strength I could find! Some of which came from my Guardian, as promised! I dashed into the trees but I knew that such would not afford me safety. The Beast would simply stomp them flat, as though they were small shrubs!

Still, it was the only thing I could think of at the moment. It bought me some time, so I <u>could</u> think. Strangely, the first thought which crossed my mind was the Beast's term of "Starchild" in reference to me. I deduced that such was because the Ultimate Evil could only view the City of Lights from a distance. From a distance, the City of Lights could easily be mistaken for a massive "star"! Hence, all the Special Ones sent to battle the Evil would be viewed by it as "Starchildren"!

The booming footsteps closing from behind, as I zig-zagged through the trees with the grace of a pro-football quarterback, almost caused me to fall from the quake-like shudder rolling beneath my feet! Somehow, I managed to maintain my balance and my momentum!

I could hear the trees cracking and crashing and being smashed to the ground by the Beast's feet, as I sensed it was uncomfortably close! I didn't know what would happen if the creature caught me and I really didn't want to find out! I didn't even want to consider such a likely possibility! I just ran and ran and ran! If this were a dream I would want to wake up screaming monster! But I couldn't wake up.

Suddenly, a huge tree fell in my path as a frighten familiar shadow fell across my position! I stopped and turned! If I had been a true human, I would have been drenched in sweat and my heart would've been pounding in my ears like the native drums that I imagined the jungle scene lacked!

I looked up, as the Beast's fire eyes ready to cook, viciously snarling, salivating face leaned close and its clawed hand with razor sharp nails ready to slice and dice was poised perhaps fifty feet above me! Ready to strike!

"Now I have you, puny Starchild!" the telepathic voice rumbled through my forethoughts, as I found myself subconsciously praying for some sort of sign as to how I could escape! How I could fulfill my "mission"!

Then, just as the situation seemed utterly hopeless and I had no doubt telepathically screamed my need for help to my Guardian. Felt a strange tingling sensation coursing throughout the exterior of the "shell" encasing my essence. One that traveled instantaneously from fingertips to the top of my head to the tips of my toes. Every square inch of that pseudo-physical exterior was experiencing the curious sensation. As though every metaphysical particle were undergoing some sort of transformation to something totally different.

Though it all probably occurred in the space of seconds, it seemed as though I were experiencing it in slow motion! Much the way some people remember an automobile accident in which they were involved. Though I was already small, my size shrank further. Becoming much leaner and sleeker. My hands became paws and my arms forelegs with spot-covered fur. My legs and feet followed suit and I could feel a tail swooshing mischievously behind me. My ears relocated themselves atop my head and became incredibly sensitive to sound. As was my nose sensitive to smells, as it twitched curiously at the end of my snout.
I was no longer a little girl! I was a Cheetah!

Perfect! As the Earth's fastest land animal, I would be able to easily out-distance and outmaneuver this monstrosity! I leaped and jumped out of his claws while he was stun with amazement of my transformation. I felt amused at the bewildered expression on the Beast's horrid face, as I stood on all fours and mentally thanked the Guardian for aiding me. Then, as the shock of what had happened passed, the creature bellowed its angered disapproval, as its voice once again assaulted my forethoughts. He ran after me far deep into the jungle where he had never been. It must have been miles and miles. I could see he was lost in the deep jungle.

"Nooo!! You are too young a Starchild to be able to Shape-Shift! Very few of your kind, that I have fought, were able to do it! This is unfair!"

"That's funny", I telepathically chuckled in an insolent tone, "You consume Lost Souls with no mercy or remorse and you speak of fairness! You just can't admit that this Starchild is more of a match for you than you expected!"

His vainity insulted and his rage fueled, the Beast howled, "I shall destroy you!"

With all its satanic might, the abomination brought its clawed hand down with more than enough force to crush whatever stood below. If I had still been standing there!

I imagined the look of surprise as the Beast's huge hand plunged into the ground beneath the underbrush. As I sprinted away with the agility of the Cheetah I Quickly achieving a speed exceeding 60 miles-per-hour and zig-zagging around trees with the grace of a pro-football quarterback!

Though I was not truly a Cheetah, anymore than I was not truly in my own body earlier, I still felt as though I were! I could "feel" my new legs flexing and stretching with more potential power and enhanced reflexes than any human! I could "feel" my claws digging into the earth in order to afford me ultimate traction, so as not to lose any speed!

I could "hear" the wind whistling past my ears the way a motorcyclist without a helmet might at the same velocity!

I could "smell" the various scents carried on the air of the humid jungle! One such scent sickeningly familiar: The stench of a million rotting corpses!

I knew the Beast was attempting pursuit, even before I felt the ground shutter with his every booming footstep or before the howls of hate which echoed into the distance!

I "smelled" him!

The cracking and snapping of trees being smashed beneath the Beast's feet touched my cat-ears, but I knew I had no reason to fear. For the creature could not hope to catch me in that animal-form! My speed and maneuverability were just too great for something so massive to match! In one brief second, I had changed my course several times! Whooshing effortlessly about the thick population of trees that comprised the Jungle of Evil! Though I could not look back at the closing creature I knew I was at least a half-mile ahead. And I would be able to maintain that margin of safety almost indefinitely! I didn't believe the same could be said for the monstrosity chasing me!

Still I knew that simply evading the Ultimate Evil was not the reason for my presence in that Realm. I knew that I had to somehow switch from a defensive posture to one of offense. I would have to take the fight to the Beast!

I assumed that my ability to Shape-Shift was not limited to land animals, as I once again "contacted" my Guardian for assistance. Moments passed, as the creature's gargantuan footfalls became more rapid and the earth trembled with an increasing ferocity to signal that it was successfully reducing that margin of safety 1 Then, I felt the tingling sensation again, which preceded the first transformation.

I hoped I had chosen the right form to help accomplish my ultimate goal.

With no loss of speed, I felt "something" begin to protrude from both sides! Growing at an unbelievable rate, as my forelegs seemed to "retract"! Going inside my chest, as the fur became feathers and my hind legs became powerful, taloned feet! The fully formed wings beating against the air with an undeniable strength and sense of purpose! Lifting me up, up, up! Until I swooped skyward over the treetops to glide on the rising thermal currents of the hot jungle!

As the Beast bellowed in greater anger, I circled and looked down at the creature that towered over the trees and almost laughed at the sight of the Ultimate Evil being so suddenly helpless to carry out its threats!

I felt as proud as the majestic Eagle I had become!

"You shall not be able to maintain that form forever Starchild!", the monstrosity mentally shrieked while slashing vainly at the air with its webbed hands. "When you land, I shall be waiting to rip you apart—piece by piece!"

"Who said I would land?" I telepathically asked, as I began beating my powerful wings against the air again. Pulling myself higher and higher into the grayish mist.

Widening my circles so as to build up my speed, before doing what would catch the Beast totally unawares!

Though I took great pleasure in taunting the roaring creature far below, the time for action had come! Having accumulated speed and power in the air, I dove with all the built-up momentum I could muster! Streaking straight for the repulsive face of the reptillian "master" of the Jungle of Evil! My sharp beak poised for the planned attack and my razor-sharp beak held forward!

I could actually feel the Guardian channeling greater strength into me during my power dive, as the expression on the Beast's face denoted puzzlement over my intentions. By the time he knew what hit him—it would be too late!

A moment later, my beak and beak found their target: The soft tissue of one of the Beast's fired eye!

As I ripped through the dark membrane and swooped away, I could hear the creature's shrieks of agony and rage shatter the air! Beating my wings furiously, I managed to elude the Beast's painful swipes with its hands and achieved the relative safety of height again.

Looking back down, the extremely sensitive eyes of the Eagle-form imparted to me a strange sight! From the eye-wound inflicted by my beak and talons oozed forth a thick, black liquid which appeared, at first, to be some form of crude oil. Then I realized the true source!

It was the symbolic "blood" of millions of Lost Souls who had been devoured by the Ultimate Evil and were still trapped in the devilish bowels of the Beast! Blackened by the passage of centuries and the satanic forces that so permeated their "prison" of reptilian flesh!

My keen hearing also picked up what I believed to be moans of relief from the Lost Souls entombed within the monster. My "mission" was not to provide momentary relief. It was to free the Lost Souls from their satanic captor!

While the creature was still wounded and its thoughts muttled by blind rage, I circled to once more build up speed and momentum. Then streaked down in yet another power dive that seemed, on the surface, to be a poor decision. But which hid a greater purpose!

With its one good eye staring upwards, the Beast opened its fanged snout wide to issue forth a tumultuous roar of murderous vengeance. Precisely what I had hoped the creature would do!

Before it realized what was occurring, I swooped into its gaping maw! Diving deep into the stinking darkness beyond the ten-foot-long fangs! Swooping deeper into the Inner Realm wherein I would find the Lost Souls the Beast had devoured for uncounted decades!

Concentrating, I "willed" one last transformation into the animal-form I felt most suited for the final stage of my plan!As the seconds raced by during my dive into the blackness within the Beast, I felt myself metamorphosize! The wings swiftly retreated, as my taloned feet returned to powerful hind legs! The forelegs also returning! My beak changing into a snarling snout with a thick, long tail swishing back and forth! And, as huge paws extended sharp claws from the muscular forelegs and pointed fangs dripped with saliva, I felt the majesty of the Eagle merge into the regality of the Lion!

I roared with the royal supremacy of the "king of beasts", as I plummeted into the obsidian depths of the Beast's bowels. The Inner Realm of Evil! The hellish "prison" of millions of Lost Souls! My cat-eyes adjusted enough in the blackness to make out faint outlines of people crammed together in the steamy stench of the creature's innards. I could sense their torment. Just as I could sense their submerged hope flickering back to life at the sound of my approaching roars. Somehow, they knew that I was there to save them!

Finally, I landed on the soft surface that lined the belly of the Beast. Without a moment's hesitation, I made use of the creature's continued confusion and lashed out with claws and teeth! Cutting, ripping, and biting at the abdominal area from within! Even deep inside the monster, I could hear its shrieks of pure pain! I could feel it jerking about, as I managed to maintain my tenuous footing! Then, seconds after I began slashing, daylight flooded through the jagged holes and tears!

The overwhelming stink inside sought escape as thick puffs of steam through the openings, as I turned to fully view the Lost Souls for the first time. The white gowns they wore upon arrival to this Realm were now coated in the same black "blood" as oozed from the Beast's injured eye. Their "bodies" were emaciated and their features haggard. Much like pictures I had seen of survivors of Nazi concentration camps. Another curious parallel between the Ultimate Evil and Hitler's twisted Germany! All had eyes filled with renewed hope overshadowing a seemingly endless torment.

As they adjusted to the sudden brillance piercing the blackness, I could see the strange combination of seemingly organic surroundings and an etherial atmosphere akin to some people's concept of Limbo. Swirling "clouds" of dark color that gave off both heat and cold simultaneously. As though summer and winter had joined to create a hellish Realm of nothingness to perpetuate the collective suffering of these poor Souls!

"Come on!" I telepathically shouted to their forethoughts, while poised near the largest hole in my Lion-form. "This is your only chance! Run!"

A sudden jerk by the shrieking Beast and the sight of one of its clawed hands swooping past the ripped and torn abdomen apparently shook the Lost Souls out of their fear-induced immobility, as they almost lost their weakened balance. With a united surge, the millions within the desolate Inner Realm rushed forward. I leaped out to lead them to the first true Freedom ever experienced by the majority of emaciated Souls who would follow my Lion-form into the surrounding trees. If all went well, my "challenge" against the Ultimate Evil of this Realm would be concluded!

With all the strength of the Lion whose form I had assumed, I leapt through the gaping hole I'd made in the Beast's abdomen and led the others to the relative freedom of the trees.

I could hear them following with what little strength their depleted spirits had left, as the once-triumphant roars of the monstrosity became weakening wails of dying agony! Though I knew the Ultimate Evil could not actually "die", for it was an Eternal Force, the form it had assumed in this realm evidently could. I was the unlikely instrument of its impending demise!

As I ran, I felt the massive legs of my Lion-form tense and flex to thrust me along. Though it was not the breakneck speed of the Cheetah, it was still a far cry from what a child-form of 4 could manage.

Just after I reached the tree line, I turned to telepathically urge the Lost Souls to quicken their pace and noticed that the further they got from the Beast the less haggard they appeared. Their bodies no longer emaciated. Their eyes no longer filled with spiritual pain and lack of hope. With every few feet they covered, and more free they became!

Then I saw with my eyes what I sensed in my soul! The mighty Beast who so terrorized the Lost Souls that wound up in the Jungle of Evil was obviously vanquished! The dark-colored mists swirling out through the great wounds I had inflicted with my powerful paws. The stench of rotting corpses no longer touched my sensitive nostrils. Even the slight glint once present the fire in his eyes had vanished. The creature's muscular legs slowly began to buckle beneath its ponderous weight, as its huge arms hung limply to its sides. Its snout became slack and drool dripped from the ten-foot fangs, as its forked tongue dangled to one side. The Beast was "dying"!

I couldn't help but feel exhilarated, as the monster slowly collapsed to its knees. Then, seemingly in slow motion, crashed face-first onto the jungle floor. Crushing several dozen trees to so much splintered wood in the process. The earth quivering as the resounding "boom" rolled into the distance like a sudden crash of thunder. Killing or destroying would be the way of man. I decided while I was flying to travel as far as I could. Away from danger to the souls. I led him deep into the forest until the forest grew taller and taller. He became smaller and smaller. He became lost, and found a new home.

One last sighs issuing forth, as the Beast was no more. As the shuttering trees slowly settled back to normal and their limbs no longer rustled in the wake of the quake caused by the fallen creature, I instantly transformed back into the child-form which most closely represented my true physical existence. There was no more need for animal-forms. No more need for my Guardian's channeled strength. No more "challenge" to address. It was over. I had won without destroying the beast. As four-year-old girl I had no knowledge of killing or destroying.

As I watched and as the Lost Souls watched, the carcass of the creature slowly disintegrated. The Ultimate Evil, no doubt, to the nothingness from that it formed returning.

Then I turned to look at the Souls that I had liberated and was not surprised to see that their blackened gowns had once again become pure white. Their eyes once more displayed an inner calm and peace no living being could comprehend. Then not so expectedly, these essences faded from view. I sensed they were now en route to the City of Lights and Ultimate Peace.

Then, I heard a strange whining sound filling the air and looked up to see the Ark that had brought us to the Jungle of Evil wavering through the sky as though it were "malfunctioning".

CHAPTER 4

▼

THE RETURN

Jessica was shaking me. "Bridgetta, wake up! Your always sleeping. You go to bed early before everyone else does. You must really like to sleep". Time had gone by I was now seven. Some reason these years were not important to me. Now I can feel relief, and enjoy my life. I smiled triumphantly back in my true physical form. I knew the challenge had been successfully concluded. What will my dream or my out of body experience be tonight? I hope it won't be another nightmare that I can't awake from. I hope it's over. "I can't wait to go back to sleep tonight!" Jessica looked at me with a question mark on her face. "I can't believe you. You just woke up and you can't wait to go back to sleep! It's a beautiful day today, no school, it's summer time! It's going to be a hundred and fifteen degrease outside, the sun is bright as hell!" (Hell! I didn't want to hear that word) she said with high excitement. She always had high positive energy even on cold dark winter nights.

We started getting ready for breakfast. I could smell the tortillas my mother was making. Also I could hear sausage sizzling, and eggs frying. All the noise my other brother and sisters were making. Happy and excited about the hiking trips they where planning.

Jessica and I hurried to join everyone at the kitchen table. "Did you girl wash your face and brush your teeth?" "Yes! Mom!" Jessica answered for the both of us. It felt good to hear all the noise. Even feeling Javier poking me on my side with his elbow getting my special attention. He whispered. "Your not the same anymore. Ever since you fell off the slide you changed. Your a lot sharper". "Thanks, Javier!"

Everyone finished their breakfast and hurried to their rooms go get ready for the big hiking trips. Our friends had arrived. I am part of the big group now. There are eight of us and seven of our friends. Fifteen kids going everywhere. Some of us where in the kitchen getting jugs of water and snacks to put in out backpacks to carry with us. Sergio, being the oldest gathered the ropes and first aid equiptment. My mother made sure we had plenty of fruit and snacks. She was in a hurry to get rid us so she could have to whole day to her self to do the laundry and clean the house.

This was her time to her self. Peaceful and quite, dad left early before day break to go to work.

So we all started off toward the desert basin no trees, no grass, just limestone rocks and cactus. We headed toward the sunrise on our way back toward sunset. We didn't need a compus. All we had to do was just look at the sun. When the sun was straight up it was time for snacks. As the sun set it was time to head for home.

There was still a cool morning breeze in the air. "David!" I called to my brother as he walked by.

"Yeah, Bridgetta, what is it?" he answered with between breaths and wrestling with the rocks at our shoes as we make our way with a sigh.

You know it was meant to happen, don't you? The accident, I mean. You know there was no way to have prevented it?"

"Yeah, there was, Bridgetta!", he retorted while spinning in my direction; deep hurt in his eyes. "I knew I wasn't supposed to let you on the slide! I never had before! But, this time, I broke the rules! I broke the rules and you were almost killed! You died, Bridgetta!"

"But I didn't" I smiled soothingly, while slowly stepping closer to my brother. Love shining in my eyes.

We had been walking for hours it was almost lunchtime the sun was straight up above us. "Look, A cave!", one of the guys shouted. We all were very tired but we had enough strength to run to the cave. "WOW! It's big. I wonder how deep it goes." Javier said. We all entered the cave. Looking amazed. David said "Everyone get you flashlights". Each of us had a backpack. We got our flashlights and begin walking into the cave. We walked a small ways.

Suddenly David ahead of the group yelled "Look stalagmite and stalactites" Javier Roomed over to a passageway to the right. "Oh! My gosh! Everybody come and see! Uniforms from the Spanish war just like in the history books! Everyone was excited They put one the coats and hats made of metal. There were boxes of rifles guns swards. "You know the solders must have hidden them here after the war.

I wasn't interested in the stuff I was hungry.
"Hey! Let's eat I'm hungry!" Everyone was playing and didn't want to stop. David said in a loud voice. "Hey! Put everything down let's eat Where's the sandwiches?

Everybody stopped they all listen to David. He seamed to be the leader of the pack. They gave everyone their sandwiches. "Good sandwiches Jessica! Did you make them?" asked Jack one of our friends. He was interested in Jessica. He went over to sit by her. They were doing the little talk of their own. David came over and sat by my side. Taking one of his hands gently in mine, He continued in a soft tone, "I can't help thinking of the accident". "Stop punishing yourself, David? Why keep blaming yourself for something you had nothing to do with? If it all happened again—it'd turn out the same."

"How do I know I won't make the wrong decision again? How do I know I won't let you do something that'll get you hurt again?"

With a shrug, I matter-of-factly replied, "You don't, David. Neither do I. But I do know that you're my brother and I love you very much and always will. No matter what. And I know you love me. Other wise you wouldn't be punishing yourself so much."

With that, I threw my arms about his neck and hugged him with all the Ii could contain. He gladly reciprocated. Days of torturous self-punishment instantly melting away with the merging of our two heartbeats. A lone tear sneak-ily rolling down one cheek and dampening mine.

Though David didn't like to cry, I was sure <u>this</u> time it made him feel freed!

He got up and said, "Alright! Everybody finish eating let's get going. Put everything back where it was!" His voice echoed through the cave, Jack stood up. "Can I have this Spanish coat?" He asked. David replied. "No! It's not ours. It doesn't belong to none of us, besides it would be a curse to take something that doesn't belong to us. Take it off and put it back". Our parents taught us well.

Everyone started packing again. The boys would burp to make the girls gross out. It was their way of getting attention. We left the history behind us as we stated out the cave. We could see sunlight up ahead.

We were on our way back home. As we made our way out of the cave, we could feel the sun heat as we exit the came. "It must be a hundred and twenty degrease!" Jack yelled. He reached for his water jug and took a big gulp. I guess he isn't use to this hot weather. He must not be from around here.

"Hey! Jack where are you from?" I called out. "Not from around here, I'm from Maine. Way up Northeast". No wonder he is having a hard time. All the guys started to pick on him. "What's the matter heating getting to you?" I think the heat was getting to everyone. Everyone was getting a little stir up.

From that moment on, David seemed to have a much greater respect for me. He no longer merely looked at me as his little sister. Now he acknowledged the fact that whatever I experienced during my coma had completely changed me. He no longer felt any responsibility for the accident. He no longer regretted what had happened. Javier, on the other hand, was an entirely different matter. He was still beset with personal guilt over what had happened. Still blamed him self for an accident for which he felt solely at fault. He still believed that I would've never gotten injured had it not been for him. The pain of that guilt was still evident in his eyes. I saw it during the few times he actually looked in my direction. Unlike with David, who assumed responsibility for the accident because he was the older than, Javier truly believed that it was he who caused me to fall. I could sense that at times he wanted to hug me. But I was hard for him to show his emotion with opened arms. But he was afraid that, should he get too close, I would be injured again.

Everyone was getting all stirred up especially the boys. They liked to show off in front of the girls by picking on one of the guys. Boys at this age always do.

They started on Jack since he was new to the group and they wanted to know more about him. He was the target. "Hey! Jack, What's your last name?" (Looking for something to pick on) Jack innocently responded.

"Ronald". To his surprise the boys started their little childish games. Marco was also interested in Jessica but no one had a clue. He kept it hidden very well. Now was his opportunity to start on Jack. He wasn't to thrill about Jessica interest in Jack.

He quickly jumped in. "Ronald or Donald like Donald Duck, Quack! Quack! Quack! Ha! Ha! Ha!" Everyone started to laugh. Just joking around. This was their way of having some fun. They all had a good sense of Humor. Not knowing that Jack took things a little personal and was getting offended. He was new to the group. He turned to Marco trying to stay in control of the situation. With a frown and said, "Marco be quite!" Marco just laughed as everyone else did.

Jessica trying to defend Jack spoke out. "Alright! You guys stop it! Making fun of some one isn't cool. So, stop it". "Oh! Jessica! You just don't want us to have any fun because you like Jack". Marco replied. Trying to get out if Jessica really did like Jack. But she didn't respond. Marco wanted to get some kind of response. He picked up a small rock and through it at Marco and Hit Him on the head and started Laughing. "Ha! Ha! Ha!" Marco turned quickly and picked a rock threw it at Marco. It began a rock fight between them.

David didn't like the rock fight. He interrupted the conflict between to two. "Hey! You guys stop it right now before some one gets hurt! We're all most home. Now Quite!" I yelled to get attention. "Look I can see the house over there! We're not far from home. I started to run with my heavy backpack hanging down from my shoulder.

I didn't know that Marco threw a big rock at same time. I started to run. All of a sudden I fell to the Ground. I was not aware I was hit. My face was in the gravel rocks I tried to get up. As I did the ground begin to move like I was on the marry-go-round. I started yelling "The ground is moving! Hold on! I can't get a hold of anything!" My fingers digging in the gravel of the line stone rocks, reach through to the dirt, struggling, digging in the dirt. I started screaming. The ground was getting faster and faster like on the marry-go-round. I was scared, screaming louder. "I can't hang on! I was crying and yelling. I could see from the side of my face the shoes of everyone. They were all standing around me but I couldn't hear them.

David ran to me. Javier just looked down at me in the state of shock. "Look at her I can't touch her she moving to much! Something is wrong?" Marco ran to see. He was scared. He cried out. "I'm sorry, I didn't mean it. I didn't know she was going to run in front. I was just trying to throw it to miss Jack. I wanted to scare Jack! I am sorry!" Tears began falling down his pudgy cheeks crying. He was not afraid to let the other boys see him cry.

Everybody just stood around me. No one knew what to do, until I passed out. David picked me up and carried me the rest of the way home. "What are we going to tell mama?" Jessica cried out with tears in her eyes. Javier cried out poor Bridgetta, she's not dead again! I don't want her to die!" David responded. "No! She's still breathing. I think she'll be ok! Shop worrying Javier!"

They reached the house, David took me to my bed and put me down on my bed. Mother was busy doing laundry she heard the gang enter the house. She yelled. "Supper not ready yet! Put everything away. Get ready for supper in a few minutes!"

Everybody gathered in the garage. "I hate to leave now. I have to go home it's almost dark. My mom doesn't want me out after dark. Be sure and call me and let me know how Bridgetta's doing!" Marco said in a very soft tone. "Yeah, David. Call me too". Jack was very concern.

The ground was moving round and round. I kept digging in the ground. A root wrapped around my left ring finger. I looked at my left hand. I grabbed tight trying to hold on. Then my left hand I could feel the roots. At last I was hanging on tight. Moving with the ground round and round, faster and faster. Darkness was around me I couldn't see anyone. I was now covered with water. Hanging on tight. The ground was moving like the ocean.

I looked at my fingers, the root turned into a golden ring with sharp jagged edges across it. Then all my fingers had rings. The movement was slowing down. The rings spread down to my wrists like a golden bracelets with jagged edges sharp as a razors. I lifted on hand but like magnetic force back to the ground or a boat or something I couldn't tell. I was shackled to something. Out from a distance appeared a woman in a white gown. She floated closer to me, behind her was a ship. "So you're the one who has taken my place I came to present you this ship. It's yours now. This is your ship. In a telepathic way.

Out From under me rose the beast that I had fought and won. He looked at me said telepathically. "I belong to you. In this dimension there is no death just defeat. I am yours Master!" I looked into his eyes they were green with specks of yellow. The woman and the ship were close enough. My golden rings and bracelets with sharp jagged edges broke free from behind the beast that I was hooked on. I climb from his back to his shoulders. The ocean was calm. I could see the ship. I answered, "There isn't anybody in the ship? Where is everybody? Am I going to be all-alone in this big ship? That won't be any fun. What good is a ship with no one to play with?

It was still dark around me. I was like glow in the dark, like a neon light. I walked around the ship I could hear the water splashing on the boat. It was so quite I could here my footstep in silence. The woman walked beside me and said. "There is not anyone on here because you have to find your own friend to bring to the ship. You decide whom you want on the ship. It's your ship!" "It's so quite hear." I replied, "It's time for you to go back to bring back some of your positive energy friends. No weapons are allowed. She laughs when you die you cant bring them with you. We both laughed "Ha! Ha! HA!" I closed my eyes when I laughed so hard.

"Bridgetta, Wake up, your laughing in your sleep!"

Javier was shaking me to wake me up. He was laughing. "Your so funny laughing in your sleep. What's you dream about I want to laugh too. Everybody Bridgetta's awake. She was laughing in her sleep. Tell us what's so funny?" Javier sat next to me to hear what I had to say. Everybody entered the room to see why Javier was to excited. They all gathered around my bed to listen. I looked at everybody. (No! they wouldn't understand!) "Javier woke me up I don't remember!" "Ahh! Bridgetta! Why won't you tell us! You never tell us your dreams. Like it's some kind of secret or something! We all ways tell you ours!" I frowned, "I can't I don't remember!" Everyone left the room with disappointment. Javier stopped at the doorway and turned back and said. "Will you tell us one of these days?" I looked and smiled. "Yeah, one of these days!"

My mom yelled from the kitchen. "Bridgetta! Come and eat your breakfast. It's getting cold. It's not good when it's cold. Hurry up!" I could hear everybody at the breakfast table whispering so my mother couldn't hear. There were so much noise mother was always busy cooking and making sure everyone had their breakfast she couldn't even hear the whispers. "I'm glad Bridgett woke up this morning". Javier whispered to Jessica. "I prayed last night for her, I was scared. Were you?" Jessica patted Javier on the head. "Yes, We all were. We all prayed for her. The creator is watching over us. Now eat!"

I entered the kitchen and sat next to David. It was the only empty chair. My mother placed the plate of eggs potatoes I love and hot tortilla. Everything smelled so good I was so hungry. Jessica watching me eat She started laughing. "Look at Bridgetta, She's eating like a starving horse. She always goes to bed early last night she was so tired of the hiking trip she went to sleep early and missed supper!" She was trying to cover up the incident. Everybody laughed but mom She said, "Alright kids finish you breakfast. I need to clean up. Girls wash to dishes it's your turn and boys sweep the floor when the girls are finished with the dishes. I'm going to finish cleaning the house".

Everybody's making so much noise as always they didn't hear Marco knocking at the door. "Hey!" He yells through the kitchen. Nobody notices. So he walks in with all the noise going on. Jessica notices. "Hi, Marco! Come and eat some breakfast with us!" Marco walks over to me with red eyes. "Are you Ok!" he whispered. He must have cried all night you could tell. "Yes!" I whispered back. Javier busted out. "Hey! Marco, you should have been here this morning, Bridgetta was laughing in her sleep. It was so funny! Have you ever laughed in you sleep?" Everybody was laughing again. Trying to cheer up Marco. They knew he was troubled.

David motioned to Marco to go over there. Marco walks over to the other side of the table where David was. David whispered. "We didn't tell mom of the incident. We were too afraid. So don't say anything. She would get upset and not let Bridgetta go hiking with us again if she knew. So be quite about it". "Ok!" Marco trying feels better about the whole situation. He walked over to me and rubbed my head. He felt the big bump on my head. "oh! I'm so sorry! And kissed me on the head". I laughed. "I'm ok! Lets go to the playground and play. Come on you guys!"

I headed towards the door. Jack was standing there. "Hi, Jack!" "Hi, Bridgetta I came over to see you. Are you Ok?" Marco was right behind me, smiled at Jack and rubbed my head she's a tuff girl. We're going to the playground come with us. "What about the other girls? Are they coming too?" Jack wanted to see Jessica. "No! They have to do the dishes. They'll come when they are finished. Then the boys have to leave the playground to sweep and mop. Let' go play!

I didn't want to get on the marry-go-round. I had enough of that spinning around. I could get on the slide I was bigger now. It doesn't bother me as much. I just want to have fun. But I could tell Javier didn't get on the slide as much. I walked over to Javier

"Javier, you are my brother and I love you with all my heart. Just as I do with David and Jessica. What I am going to say is coming <u>from</u> my heart. Please, believe what I say. You, Javier, were not at fault for the accident. No one was. It was meant to be. Do you understand? It would've happened no matter what. No one blames you for what happened. No one holds you responsible for the fall. Not me, David, or Jessica. Not Momma and Poppa. No one but you, Javier and you don't have to be afraid to play with me. You're not going to be the cause of me to get hurt. I promise."

Javier stopped his tears and stared deeply into my eyes, as though being held in some sort of hypnotic hold. I smiled and continued in a tone of total love.

"The only person who is punishing you for something that wasn't your fault, Javier, is you. And the only person who can forgive you—is you. Please, believe in yourself enough to forgive yourself. And be my brother again." Javier's eyes suddenly denoted incredible relief, as he returned my smile with one of his.

Time passed by, now I was going to junior high for my seventh year of school.

I was excited; I was now going up changing into adolescences at the age of 13.

My first day in school there was a boy named Johnny in my homeroom class. Everyone joked about him. They said he was strange. I didn't think so, But there again they would think I was strange too, if they knew about what I have been through. I looked at the boy; I began to like him He wasn't so strange to me, in fact I thought everyone was strange because I was Indian but you couldn't tell, because I had light brown hair and very light skin. I was always mistaken for being white. I wanted to be dark like my brothers and sisters. I couldn't change what I am.

It was lunchtime, I went to the cafeteria got my tray and looked for a place to sit. It was packed. I walked around found a place in a corner and sat down. There was a empty chair beside me. It was less crowded.

"Hi, Is this chair taken? My name is Nicole! Can I sit here?" she asked with a smile.

"Yes, you can sit there". I said.

She replied, "What's your name?"

"Bridgetta".

"This school is a bigger than I thought it would be. It's different than grade school. We have to change rooms for different subjects". She was making conversations. I didn't say much just eating my lunch. "Bridgetta! Would you like to be my friend? Hang around together?" School just started you're my first friend. How about it?"

I looked at her. "Alright, I guess so".

"Do you walk home? I do".

"No! I take the buss. I live across the street from my old elementary school."

"Do you live in Loving?" She said.

"Yes" "I just moved right outside of Loving, Hey, we can visit after school. What do you say?" Can we be friends?"

"Yes, I guess so" I finished my lunch. I'll see you around". I got up and headed to my next class. Johnny was in my next class. I sat two desks behind him, so I could watch him. I didn't want him to know I liked him. I wanted to keep a distance.

As time went by Nichole and I started to hang around together at school and after school.

The phone rang. Javier answered. "It's for you Bridgetta"

I picked up the phone. "Hello" "Hi, Bridgetta I'm going to the store. Would you like to come along? I'll stop by your house". "Wait let me ask my mom" My mom was doing laundry. The washing machine makes a lot of noise so I had to talk a little loud. "Mom! Can I go with Nichole to the store?" She was gathering clothes together.

"Yes But don't stay gone to long"

"Thanks, mom" I ran back to the phone. "It's ok with my mom. I'll see you in a little while. Bye!"

Nichole knocked at the door. I opened it and we went walking to the store. "Bridgetta, I like being your friend" We walked by a gift stop. "Let's stop and look around in this store" Nichole said.

"Alright" I said.

We walked around there were so many different things. "Look, Bridgetta come over here" I walked over to were she was at. She was look-ing at some rings. "Do you like these rings?" She asked me. "Yea, they are neat looking"She picked up two of them and handed me one. "Try it on" I tried it on. "Does it fit?"

"Yes, it does" I said. She looked at me and smiled. "You want to be my close best friend. Don't you?"

"Yea, I replied.

"Well! This is test to be my friend. You have to take the ring and walk out the door!" I hesitated. She was going out the door. Everything happened so fast I wasn't thinking. I went out the door. We left the store. She gave me a big hug and said. "You're my best friend, we both have a ring alike.

I didn't feel very proud. I felt sick. I tried to smile and be happy but I couldn't. We went walking home. She left my home happy, but I wasn't I've never done anything like this before. My hands were shaking, I took the ring off and put it under a rock under the steeps. It was dark and everyone was getting ready for bed.

"Bridgetta, Is that you?" "Yes, Mom" I was scared for what I had done I didn't want to talk or be around anyone. Everyone was so busy they didn't even notice me.

That night I couldn't get to sleep. Voices kept going through my head. "You could go to jail if you got caught, you could go to hell" I knew it was wrong but it was to late I had already done it. "I am going to hell". Tears fell from my face, I couldn't get to sleep. Over and over thoughts going through my mind. I looked at the clock. 12:00 then 1:00 2:00 every hour kept going by like days. I just toss and turned. I was shaking. I couldn't get to sleep. I have to go to school in the morning. I can't sleep. I felt horrible. The sun began to come up through my window. Everyone was getting up for breakfast and then off to school.

"Bridgett! Come and eat your breakfast! Hurry! Don't miss your buss!" My mom cried out. I washed my face and got dressed. I went to the table and sat down. "What's wrong with Bridgetta! You look sick!" Javier cried out over all the noise everyone was making. Everyone stopped to look at me. I put my head down. I couldn't face anyone. My mother came over to me. Put her hand on my face. "What's wrong?" I looked at her with guilt and a tear fell from my eye. "Everyone get going, Bridgetta staying home she looks very sick". I couldn't eat one bite of food or drink one drop of juice. I got up with my head down walked back to my room. "Bridgetta! Let me finish the dishes I'll be up to see about you".

I layed in my bed staring at the ceiling. My mom opened the door and sat on my bed beside me. "What's wrong Bridgetta?" I got up from my wet pillow of tears. She looked at me wiped the tears from my eyes held me in her arms. "Have you been crying all night?" My voice trembled.

"Yes, Mom I did something wrong. I knew it was wrong. I did it anyway. It happened so fast" She looked into my red eyes full of tears.

"Tell me what happened?" I told her what Nichole and I did. "Where is the ring?" She asked. "I'll go with you to return it and you have to tell the owner what you did".

We arrived at the gift shop. My Mom asked for the owner. He come out of his office. "My baby girl has something to say to you. Go ahead Bridgetta"

I looked at the man and trembled. "I took this ring and I want to give it back. I am very sorry I've never done this before. I couldn't sleep last night. I was wrong. I want to make everything right again".

The man looked at my mom said. "You have a little brave girl with strong carriage to face her crime" He turned to me and said. "Thanks for returning the ring. It's a three dollar ring but the price of courage is to return is priceless". He knelled down and gave me a hug patted me on the back. "You will be a fine girl". My mother was proud of the lesson I had learned. She knew it was tuff.

We returned home. "Now, I want you to go get some sleep! Do you feel better now that you got everything straight?" "Yes, mom" I said with a deep breath and a sigh of relief. I changed the pillowcase with a nice clean smell.

I had sleep until the next morning for school. I now had to face Nichole at lunchtime. The bell rang for lunch I hurried to the cafeteria. I was almost the first in line. I got my lunch as quick as I could. I didn't even go to my locker kept my backpack on until I got to the table. There was a lot of places to sit I never realized how easy it to find a place to sit. Half way threw my meal the cafeteria was quickly packed. One last gulp of my milk and on my way. I picked up my tray, headed toward the door when entered was Nichole. "Hi, Bridgettia! Are you leaving? Where have you been I've been looking for you! I herd you were sick yesterday! Look she whispered I got my ring on! Where's yours? At home?" "No" I answered. "I've have to catch up on some of my school work I missed out on yesterday. See you around. Bye!" With a question look on her face. "Alright".

The last bell at the end of the day rang. I hurried down the steps and tripped on the last step. "Are you alright Bridgettia?" my books sliding on the floor. I looked up and there was Johnny kneeling down to help me pick up my books.

"Oh! What a mess I made, my papers, my book!" Embarrassed, I felted my face turn red a apple.

It's ok! I'll help you. The halls were getting more and more crowded making it hard to collect some of my papers.

"Thanks! Johnny" My heart was melting very fast as Johnny was getting closer and closer as the crowd pushing and shoving the both of us. We finely gathered everything. "Here's the last paper. I think we got everything." We both looked down to the floor at the same time, bumped our head together real hard. "Ouch!" We both said at the same time. We laughed as the crowd shoving Back and forth tighter and tighter. It was like being on a boat rocking back and forth trying to keep our balance.

"Can I walk you to your locker?" He asked.

With out hesitation. "Sure! We were making our way through the crowd like ping pong table. Finely make it to my locker it was getting less crowded. A lot more room everyone was leaving the school. The halls was getting less crowded. We had more room to move around.
"Thanks Again!" I said with a big smile of delight.

"Anytime! I'll see you tomorrow!" He had a nice smile too.

"Ok!" With a deep breathe and sigh as he left down the hall. I turned to unlock my locker. I Lost track of time with all the commotion. I looked at my watch. I had missed the buss. I was getting ready to close my locker door when suddenly Nichole appeared.

"Hi, Bridgettia. I haven't had a chance to see you to day. I missed you today!" Almost everybody had left the school. "Bridgettia! I saw you walking with Johnny. Do you like him?"

"No!" With a smile I couldn't help. "We're just friend".

"Well! Good! You're my best friend and no one comes between us!" I was in a question mark. Everyone had left. The hallways were empty and the lights had just turned off. You could only see the sunlight down the hall coming threw the glass doors. I didn't know what to expect next. "Bridgett! All the boys like my boobs. They think I'm sexy. Do you?" She had large breast, I never gave it any thought. MY sister had large breast. We were all created differently. I was small. I Didn't think there was an issue.

"Sexy? I don't think of you as sexy to me, maybe to the boys, not me!" I looked at her with a frown.

She smiled and said. "Sure you think I'm sexy!" She grabbed my hand and put it on her breast. "Feel them!"

I jerked my hand away. I was very upset. I lost control. I quickly grabbed her by her throat with both hands my books fell to the floor. "You're an evil person!" I pushed her against the lockers three times. "Your evil! Your evil! You got me to steal a ring! I had to take it back. I am not a thief. You're a thief! Your evil! You are not my friend! You are not my friend! Now this! You are evil!" I was choking her. Her face was turning colors. I heard my mane called. "Bridgetta! What are you doing?" I looked beside me. There was a spirit standing in the dark. Time stood still. I turned to the spirit. "she an evil person. She does evil things. She should die!" Tears fell from my face. I cried out. My spirit left my body.

I turned to the spirit, Confused. "Who are you?" He had on a white robe. "I've never seen you before? Who are you?"

He reached his hand out to me. "I was sent by our father to come down and explain to you. Our father cannot come down to this demention. I can." "you can come here and go up there too. Just like me except you're a spirit. Were you in a physical form like me?" There was so much love in his eyes. "Yes, my child, my physical form had died. Now I live in the spirit. Where are you now?" He asked me. "I am here!" "Yes, She is evil, but she belongs here you don't. This is her World not yours. You have the universe she doesn't. You must let her go. There is good and evil in this world we cannot interfere. We cannot kill. If we do we are evil too and have to stay here until the right time. This world is on it's way to self destruction of evil.

I fell to my knees. I cried out. "I don't want to be here. Hot burning Tears running down my checks. "I don't want to be in this evil world". I pounded my hand on the floor. "Please, I don't want to be here" I cried again. He reached down to me. I looked up and reached for his hands. "Why do you have holes in your hand?" Tears of pain in my heart felt his pain. "Did you die with holes in your hand?" I stood up "You must have had far more pain than I did?" I was now crying for the pain he must have gone through. "Oh! Please forgive me! Tears running down my face faster then ever". I am so selfish. "Please, Forgive me! I understand now. I want to be a good person". Tears fell from his beautiful eyes down his cheeks and rolled off his beard. He wrapped his arms around me to comfort me. His robe was like the wings of my father.

My eyes blinked. I could see Nichole's face turning purple. I threw her to the floor. She was gasping for air.

Coughing and choking for her breathe. I looked at my watch it was just two minutes. I know time must have stopped.

Nichole got up off the floor crying gathering her books. She ran down the hall to the double glass doors. There were no more tears on my face. There was no pain. I felt a peace within me. I gathered my books and walked down the hall all I could hear was my foot steps. When I reach the double glass doors. I heard a voice say. "Bridgetta! You're a special one!" I looked up through the glass doors up into the sky my voice echoed in the halls.

"I Love you father! I know I'll see you again!" I opened the glass doors looked up to the sky. I know I could see you threw the clouds with a smile.

"Bridgetta!" "Bridgetta!" Javier yelling. "Hey! Bridgetta!" I turned. I was going the wrong way. Like I was in a trans. I snapped out of it quickly before anyone would notice. Javier came running toward me. "You didn't get off the bus. We knew you missed the bus. Why did you miss the bus?" we were walking toward the car. Everyone was in the car like always. Everybody always stayed together. Everyone was talking and laughing at me because I missed the bus. They were making fun of me. I laughed with them and I smiled. "I lost track of time"

"Alright! Quite down" My mother had to yell with all the noise. She started up the car and headed home.

When we got home everyone ran into the house and into the kitchen. Jessica said "we didn't get to eat we had to wait until we came back from getting you. Are you hungry? I'm starving" "Come to think of it, yes"

We were the last to sit down at the table. Mom was getting the baked chicken out of the oven. When the phone ring. Jessica got up from the table "I'll get it!"

Mom put the baked chicken in the center of the table. "Who is it?" She said. With all the noise we couldn't hear Jessica talking. We just waited until she came back.

Everyone was talking at the same time, eating, passing the food around the table.

Jessica returned to the table. Mom! Telephone. Do we know anyone in the reservation? My Mom looked surprised. "Yes, You guys have a great grandfather who is my mothers father. Oh! My dear!" She went for the phone. We looked at each other. We didn't know we had a great grandfather. "Wow! He must be real old!" Javier said. "I wonder what He looks like?" I said. Just then mom came to the table. Well kids we have to go to the reservation. Your great grandfather is going to die. We have to leave tomorrow morning. I'll have to call the school.

"How come we never got to visit our great grandfather?"

"Well! Kids I have a story to tell eat while I tell you the story. When my mother was four years old they lived on a farm. In 1905 The white man came to the land and wanted our farm. There were a lot of fighting among the Indians and the white man. My grandmother and grandfather didn't know what to do. So they had a meeting with all the tribe of the land. A big ceremony was held. This ceremony was the biggest ceremony in our history.

There were thousands that gathered. A ritual was held.

The first night we had to be cleansed by a smudging ritual. This ceremony the chief would perform. We built a big fire in the center of the circle of the people. He had the sacred words to clean our spirits in order to enter the sacred grounds. What this does is get rid of the negative energy within us and be full of positive energy. It takes all night to perform. The second night we dance the sacred dance and sing the sacred song. We bring positive energy up to a higher level with out song and dance. The third night we call the spirits down and we ask them question. Well! My great grandfather is the Indian chief. He passed it down to my grandfather.

They went to the spirits with their problems with the white man. The spirits came down. They said, "This is not our world to claim. Why do we want this world when it belongs to the evil? We have the whole universe after we leave this world. This world is very short. The universe is eternity! We have to be civilized. Come to an agreement without bloodshed. Be the one to die not the one to kill!" This message was told to all the tribes but some of the tribes didn't want to be civilized. Some of us wanted peace. When we came back to the land we made a peace agreement. We had to pay our taxes, change our names and latter gave us numbers. We had to work the farm until for 50 years to claim homestead. In 1910 they signed the papers. New Mexico became a state. My mother was then nine years old. Some of the Indians didn't they made a reservation.

Fifteen years ago our great grandfather went to the reservation to become the chief. Now he is sick and they have to appoint a new chief. We are going to the reservation and to the ceremony. We are going to take part of everything so be ready.

We all were very quite and listening to my mothers story. When the door opened. It was my father coming home from work. "WoW! I've never seen this house so quite in my entire life. What's going on here?" He looks around at everybody. "Moms telling us a story dad." said Adrian. "He already knows the story". "What story?" With a question look on his face. "The story was about the peace agreement with the white man. "What brought that all up?"

My dad asked. "My grandfather is sick and won't make it! We have to go to the reservation tomorrow!" "Alright! But the burial ceremony is different. You all will find out what a real Indian is all about. Get ready for a big event coming up. Now everybody get up do the dishes and clean up. Get to bed early we got big time coming up.

The next morning my mom came to get us all up and packing for a week. The sun was barely coming up over the horizon. We hurried with breakfast. Mom fixed sandwiches and snack for the long trip to the reservation. Everyone was tired and sleepy. We slept the first two hours. One by one everyone started to wake up. "How much longer till we get there?" Alicia said in a sleepy tone. My dad was in deep meditation being hypnotized by the long straight road. "Dad! How much longer!" This time in a louder voice.

"Oh! I'm sorry! In about four more hours!" "Wow! That's a long time. I woke up the silence was broken now. I sat up and looked out the window watching the desert plants swish by. Sergio woke up and said. "Dad! Do you think Great grandpa will be alive when we get there? I hope so I want to hear some stories." "Yes I hope so. Your mother can tell you some of his stories." Looking in the rear view mirror. "Tell us some stories mom."

"That's a good idea Sergio! It will make time pass by quicker. Since we are headed north I'll tell you the story about the Rock with wings. Very close to the reservation there is a place called Four Corners, an area where four states meet. During the time when the white man tried to take our land. There were a large number of different tribes at the time. The white men came to kill the Indians and take the land. All the different tribes knew of this large mountain it was one big sacred rock. The creator controls this rock. When the white man came to destroy our people, they had succeeded killing many tribes. When they came all the different tribes gathered around. The land was flat and you could see big clouds of dust coming far away. We had to gather what we could and run to the big rock. There were very few horses we had to carry what we could and run by foot. It was five to ten miles to the rock. It looked close but so far away. To this day only the Creator protected us. We couldn't have done it with out our Creator. They could see the soilders were far away. As time was gaining on them, the soilders were getting closer and closer. All the tribes made it to the mountain they chanted and chanted the sacred word of meditation. The rock begin to shake. A child was running and crying to the rock trying to make it. You could sill hear the child crying mommy! Mommy! A warrior from another tribe ran to rescue the child. He reached down and grabbed the child and ran to the mountain. Everyone held their breath for the child. Just as the warrior made it to the big mountain rock. The shaking and the vibration broke lose from the ground. They stood at the edge of the rock as it lifted seventeen hundred feet off the desert floor and was visible from a hundred miles away. The tribes watched below as the solders fired their rifles up toward the rock round and round but no avail. Some of the tribes disappeared, and some still remain of the reservation, and some like us homestead our land. We had to change our names, latter were given numbers. They say they killed us but we know better.

"Are we going to see this big mountain rock?" I asked quickly. "Yes! Bridgetta!" My mom and dad smiled at each other. Knowing I loved true mysterious events. "What about you dad do you have any stories to tell?" Dad looked in the rear view mirror. "I do but you must not tell anyone this story because they won't understand. I don't understand. I'll still tell you kids this story."

"Is it as good as mom's story?" Adrian asked. "Yes, it's as good as mom's story!"

"My brothers and I were working on the farm. There were nine of us. My one sister was helping mother with supper. My dad was putting the horses in the barn. We still had to work in the fields until my dad said to stop. The sun was going down and it was getting dark. We would yell at father. "It's getting dark we can't see!" We wanted to stop but we couldn't. My dad heard us and yelled back. "Keep working! Don't stop!" So we kept trying to work in the dark. I looked up above the fields watching the sun barely peeking over the fields. When all of a sudden I saw this light like a ball bouncing up and down. "Look!" I pointed to the ball bouncing. "Look! What is that?" My brothers stopped working they looked in silence. We were in shock, in a question mark. We didn't know what to do. We just stood there and watched as it came closer and closer. My oldest brother screamed out loud. "It's a ball of fire! There are three of them. There coming this way! Quick grab shovels and whoa rakes, anything. We have to put it out before it burns up our crop. We all started running toward the ball of fire. We got closer and closer. My older brother seem to tell us what to do. We just did it. "Quick! Make a circle! Hit it with our shovels and rakes, put it out!" We started to hit it and two jumped up high up above us. The smaller one couldn't go very high.

We started hitting it. Suddenly we heard a noise of crying. I yelled. "Stop it! Stop it!" We're hurting it! Stop!" Everybody stopped. We stood there and looked. We steeped back and watched. It was crying like a child. Leave it alone. Let it go! I said. One of my brothers wanted to strike it again. I grabbed his hand and said, "No! I'll beat you up it you strike it again. Let it go!"

We all back away from it to let it go. You could hear it crying and trying to bounce back toward to other two fireballs. "Look! It's a mom, dad and baby!" We were sad for what we did. Tears fell down our cheeks. The next morning we told our mom and dad. They didn't believe us. So we took them to the place hoping to find burn spots on the tumbleweeds, cactus or bushes. To our surprise there was nothing burnt? My dad got made at us. "Alright! enough of your foolishness. Go back and work on the farm." We never did know what it was but never talk about it again. I still hurt every time I think about it. I hope the little one was alright? I feel guilty sometimes when I think about it?" A tear feel from my dad's eye. He was holding back his feeling.

"Wow! Dad, that was a good story. Was that really true?" Adrian asked. "Yes! That's why I asked you guys not to tell anyone. Nobody would believe it." He turned to mom. "Enough stories, how about a sandwich and a drink. Everybody hungry?" We all yelled. "Yea, Let's eat we're hungry!" My mom got out the sandwiches and drinks. We ate in the car saving some time on the road.

After everyone ate their lunch we just sat in silence for a while. It didn't last very long. "How much longer" Jessica asked breaking the silence. We should be there in a short time. Look you can see the Rock with wing now. Up ahead can everyone see it?" Everyone looked straight ahead as we watch this rock sitting at a great distance. It's here that the rich past is a visually pervasive as the surrounding country. It was sitting in the flat desert floor. "We are still a hundred miles away. We'll reach it in a couple of hours then the reservation is just on the other side." My dad said. We were hypnotized by this rock watching it getting bigger and bigger as we came closer and closer. It's sculptured sandstone, red-walled canyons and ancient dwellings. Its silence wonders speak to us with a certain elegance. We watched this rock turn into a huge mountain before our eyes. Can we climb the mountain?" I asked. "No we don't have time." My mother said. It wasn't to much longer as we turned to watch the mountain behind the car. We then watch out of the rear window. "Look ahead you can see the reservation." My dad cried out loud with excitement. It looked like a small village with adobe houses. We turned left on a dirt road. The dust started flying like a cloud of smoke trailing our way to the village. We drove passed a few houses. Then stopped at house in back of the village. They had horses. My dad turned the engine off. We started getting out of the car one by one. You could now hear the pigs in the pin, then the chickens started greeting our arrival. "Hello!" A man came out of the house with a big smile. He had long braided hair with a touch of gray. Then a older woman who had a hard time walking. "Hello!" My mom and dad were greeted with big hugs and smiles. They were talking in the Indian language. We didn't understand what they were saying. They didn't speak English. They reached down and gave each of us a hug and then a big kiss on the cheek. We entered the small adobe house.

Some of us had to sit on the cracked linoleum floor. We didn't mind. We watched the adults speak to each other laughing and smiling. They were so happy we came. My mom came over to us and said. "Be very quite, get up and come with us to see great grandfather in the next room." We got up and walked into the next room. You could see the sun going down through the open window. The cool breeze moved the curtain back and forth. I tried to look around everybody, to see if I could see my great grandfather. I could here mom speaking in Indian. I worked my way to the bed and poked my head through the crowd. Now I could see. He turned and looked at me. He smiled very big struggling to speak in a soft tone. "What is he saying?" I asked my mom. "He asked me if you were mine." I smiled at him and reached out and gave him a big hug and said. "You're my great grandpa!" He was so happy a tear of happiness fell from his eyes with a smile. My mom looked at us and said some more Indian words. "What did you say?" Javier asked.

"He said, I have a good looking tribe. He also said the number 6 child is a secreted one. Now children it's time to leave the room go back to the other room." We slowly left and sat down back on the floor. There were so many of us there weren't enough chairs. We sat there and watched my aunt and uncle and my great grandma speak the language my mom and dad knew. It was getting dark then two boys and one girl entered the house. They didn't know much English.

"Children! I want you to meet your cousins, Jimmy 16, Marques 18, and Rita 19. We said hello. It was getting late and we didn't have time to talk much. MY aunt brought out blankets and pillows we all slept in the living room we didn't mind at all.

The next morning the sun was very hot shinning through the big picture window. They didn't have air-conditioner just a fan to circulate the air. The adults were up early and the rosters were crowing morning.

Jessica was now 22, "Everybody get up and fold your blankets and stack your pillows in a pile it's time to get up! Hurry! Get up!" She always instructed everyone. Everybody pushing and shoving trying to make their way around the small living room. Everyone was anxious to be with our relatives. It was a new experience for all of us.

We all folded our blankets and took turns to the restrooms to wash our face and brush our teeth. After I left the restroom, I turned to the room where my great grandfather laid on his bed. I walked to his bedside knowing he will soon die. I watched as he slept. He seamed very peaceful. I felt comfort as I kneeled to my knees and placed my head against the bed. Tears started falling down my cheeks as I began to pray. I closed my eyes. "Guardian!" I said in silence. "I know you are always with me. I come to you for more comfort and security. I don't know my grandfather but feel as if I have known him all my life. He is very sick and I know he will be with you, and some day so will I. I will always feel your wings around me forever as if it was yesterday." Just then a pat on my head, "Hello!" My grandfather whispered. I lifted my head and wiped my tears. That was one of the few English words he knew. He began talking in the Indian language with a smile and a sparkle in his eye. I smiled with the comfort of his spirit. I could tell he was in great pain as he kept it hidden very well.

Jimmy entered the room. "Good-morning Bridgetta!, Grandfather, I brought your breakfast grandfather." They started talking in Indian.

"I'll came back later and see you grandfather" He looked at me with a smiled, nod his head. I went into the kitchen. Everybody was at the table and some were at the corner on the floor where they could find room to sit and eat. I got my breakfast and went outside to find a place to eat. I sat on a big rock and laid my drink on the dirt. I moved it around to balance it so it would not spill.

Jimmy came outside with his breakfast and sat next to me. "This is a good place to eat breakfast. Is it alright if I sit here" I smiled "Sure, It's alright". "Grandfather said you look like a little angel. I told him I think so too!" "Really! That's nice to hear. I felt a comfort from grandfather. Like I have always known him". "Yes, he is a sacred grandfather. We don't have much but his spirit was always happy. He knows he will meet with the creator soon that is why he has a sparkle in his eyes. Did you notice?"

"Yes, I did notice." Jimmy was in a good spirit. "Tonight we will have a ceremony. We will gather around the fire that represents the center of the universe. We will dance around in a circle. I'll teach you some of the dances. "Wow! I would love to learn." We are going to have a smug that we cleanse our spirit for the next sacred ceremony the 2nd night. Every night we dance to welcome the spirits to gather around the fire. This is a ritual that is practiced for centuries. Our ancestors kept this ceremony a secreted only in the reservation. The outside world wouldn't understand or know anything about it they have a great fear of the unknown. Their mind is closed and locked away and receive very negative energy that will keep them separated from the positive energy. That's why we have a smug ceremony to purify our mind and spirits." I looked at Jimmy with concern for my family. "Does my family know all this?" Jimmy replied. "Your dad and mom know. They are telling you brothers and sisters right known so they will be aware when the ceremony begins. We will dress up with customs and paint our faces." I was very excited. "Do you think I can dress up too?" He laughed. "Sure, Let's ask your mom and dad if you can come with me now. Are you finished eating?" "Yes, Let's ask!" We went into the kitchen it was very quiet while my grandfather was explaining to everyone about the ceremony. Jimmy and I stood by the doorway and listened.

My grandfather had the smug sticks lit and began the prayer. Silence filled the air and my father and mother repeated some of the secreted word. Even though we didn't understand the word we could feel the sprit move around and the energy shifting among us until it became very still. We were all still with out a batting of an eye.

As my grandfather circled around the room, he smuged everyone individually with sacred words. He came over to me, then to Jimmy. He was the last. For a moment everyone waited before my father broke the silence. Your mother and I are going to visit the village and gather up our customs for tonight ceremony while all of you clean up and put the dishes away." "Father! May I go with Jimmy to look for my clothing? I want to dress up. Jimmy's going to teach me the sacred dance!" Everyone could see the excitement on my face with joy! My dad smiled and was very proud. "Sure, Bridgetta!" I grabbed Jimmy's hand. "Come on Jimmy let's go!" I just couldn't wait any longer. We headed down the dusty road. I could tell Jimmy was excited to work with me. "Let's go to my aunts house she makes a lot of different dresses you can pick out what you like. "Aunt Betty!" Jimmy yelled as we entered her house. "I am over here!" She was in the back room. We went over to the back of the house. "Hi! Auntie, This is Bidgetta Javier's youngest daughter." She smiled. With her broken English she tried to speak to me. "You very cute girl." Jimmy started gathering some dresses she had just made. "Look, Bridgetta! See if you can find something for tonight! Auntie she is going to dress up for the ceremony tonight and I'm going to teach her to dance with me!" "oh! Nice! You like! You pick one you like!" I started to go through them. "Wow! Auntie they are so beautiful, red orange, teal, purple, oh! I love the yellow with orange. I'll pick this one." Aunt Betty handed me a beaded head-band with some beautiful feathers on them. "Here, moccasins try, they fit?" I put them on.

"WOW, I look like a real Indian. I feel Great! I am ready to lean to dance. I want to surprise my family. Come on Jimmy Let's get started. My Aunt brought out the drum and began the beat. It was a beat of the heart. Jimmy started the steps and I followed. He started slow as I caught on very quickly. "You learn very quickly Bridgetta. Now try this step." It was a double time forward and backward motion. "Do it again!" This was a little tricky so he did it again. "I let's keep trying until I get it just right." He kept doing it again and again, until I got it just right. "Now" he said. He picked up a feather. "This is an eagle feather. I got it from a eagle when I went hunting with my dad. It has been blessed by the medicine man. It's a secreted feather. I'll dance in a circle then I'll place it on the ground the spirits will guide the feather around till until it settles on a peaceful ground When it does that is when you do your dance around the feather until it lifts high enough for me to start the dance with you. Then we dance with the spirits. We dance faster and faster until the feather rises high enough that I can catch it with my mouth. When I do, the dance is over with one last beat of the heart of the dance," We practiced our steps over and over again. I could feel the pain in my legs but somehow I kept going without feeling tired. It was on a constant rhythm that took control of me like up and down a roller coaster. We danced until the sun began to set. "We have to quit now Bridgetta I have to take a shower and get ready in 30 minutes. I need to put my custom on and paint my face. I'll meet you in forty-five minutes. Change and take your custom with you shower and I'll meet you at the sacred ground." "Alright, Jimmy!" My Aunt Betty help me gather my things. "Thank you very much Aunt Betty! I love my custom you made. I feel so beautiful." "I made it for you. A gift for you from me." I reach over to her and gave her a big huge and a kiss on her winkled cheek as she smiled.

I ran back to my great grandfathers house on the dusted trail. I pushed opened the screen door. "Bridgetta! Everybody is ready for the ceremony except for you quick take your shower. What do you have in that bag?" "Oh! Mother it's a surprise for everyone!" "Alright, Bridgetta You are always full of surprises. We will meet you at the ceremony. Come on kids lets go it's getting late. They carried my great grandfather to the car even if it was just a short walk he didn't have enough strength. "Oh good! I have the whole house to myself" I said to myself.

I ran to the shower quickly. It was nice not having to fight for the shower. I hurried to put on my costume. Towel-dry my hair. Put on my headband with the feathers.

I rushed to the ceremony with my moccasin still unlaced.

The ceremony had just began. I went over and stood behind the group of dancers. I tried to hide behind all the big feathers on the head dressers that the Indian Chef was wearing. All the dancers look so beautiful. The beautiful sounds of the bells on their customs. I kept looking around for Jimmy. I hope I didn't keep him to late. As the dancers started out one by one forming a single circle. I was the last one standing alone just for a moment. Just then I head a cry in the crowd. It was Jimmy in the middle of the circle. He motioned for me to come join him in the middle of the circle. He looked great! I just couldn't believe my eyes, this was happening to me. It was so perfect, it felt like a dream. I felt like I was in a trans. The moon was so bright it lit up the whole desert sky. My whole family joined in the circle everyone watched Jimmy and I in the middle of the circle around the fire that represent the center of the universe. We danced so perfectly that it seemed we danced for years of practices.

You could feel the positive energy of the spirits in the whole universe come down. When Jimmy ended our dance with the feather in his mouth. You knew the highest of spirits were among us everyone yelling and screaming with such joy. As Jimmy dance leaving to the outside of the circle as I followed everyone following behind single file until the circle unwind inside out. At the end was the Chief left standing. Then last drum beat. Silence was in the air as you could only hear the crackling of the fire. The chief then pick up the smug stick pointed down to the fire lit the smug stick and began the sacred words to welcome the spirits. Jimmy whispers to me to explain what is going on.

The Indian Chief gives each individually cleansing of sacred word. These sacred word are not allowed to be used in any other way. After He finished to the last baby. He returned to the center of the circle by the fire. You couldn't see the spirits but you could feel the spirits circle around the circle round and round spiraling upward motion toward the heavens into the stars like a light of energy. Sparks from the fire were soon disappearing as the ceremony ended. The Chief threw the last end to the smug stick. The moon was so bright as the fire slowly fading away. Everybody then talked among each other.

"Bridgetta! That was so great" Javier came up to me. You look beautiful in your costume and dance so perfectly with Jimmy." Jessica came around to Jimmy and I. "Jimmy could you teach me to dance like Bridgetta!" He laughed.

"Maybe one day!"

The next morning everybody was up and at the breakfast table. I woke up by the sound of the roster crowing at the same time. I took my shower and dried my hair. I went to my great grandfathers bedside. He was awake but very weak. "Good-morning great grandfather!" I smiled with a chance to speak to him. "Great grand-father? I feel a lot of comfort and peace with you." Jimmy entered the room. "Good-morning great grandfather and Bridgetta." "Good-morning Jimmy!" Great grandfather began talking to Jimmy in a very soft whispery struggling each word. Jimmy smiled and turned to me. "He said you danced with the spirits very well and enjoyed the watching the danced. The spirits were very pleased. You're the seventh child. A sign will come to you and a vision has crossed your path. I gave your father your name, Bridge. Meaning a spirit who travels through you with a message. You're a bridge from life to the spirits." Jimmy looked at me with surprised emotion. "Bridgetta, He says you're a chosen one? Did you know this?" I was shocked that great grandfather would Know this. "Uhhh! Great grandfather! You're the only one I can talk to about this. I have kept this from everyone fearing no one could understand." My face turned red like fire and tears began to fall from my eyes. I knelled to the floor and held his hand in my hands. "Please help me great grandfather! I've been going through all kinds of spiritual changes. I wanted so much to tell my family or somebody who would understand and guide me through life for I feel so different from everybody. I know I am not like everybody else. Sometimes I feel like I'm not human. I feel.............abnormal." I felt like a heave load lifted from me. I finely released all this energy I have kept hidden inside. I couldn't stop the tears from falling from my eye. I had a pain in my heart that throbbed so hard and loud like the drum beating at the ceremony. He said, "Don't be sad, be proud of who you are. You are a blessing. Maybe you will write a book of your journey." He tried to joke and cheer me up.

I lifted my red face full of tears. "Oh, great grandfather. I could never write a book. I'm not very good in school. {Laughing and crying at the same time} My grades aren't good. I had trouble trying to pass this year. I'm not good at all in history! I just don't understand the rest of the world!" He said, "He doesn't either and he never been to school." We all laughed. Jimmy reached down to pick me up from my knees. I looked at Jimmy. "Jimmy do we have to tell anyone?" "He said, When your ready to speak the spirits will guide you at the right time. I am here when you need me. Great grandfather has taught me well. I will take his place. The spirits have all given me a vision." Suddenly I wasn't alone anymore. "He said when the spirits come to take him to the other side. His spirit will return when we call upon him for time of need." "Oh! Thank you great grandfather. I know the after life. "You will be where I wish I could be. A far far better place. We will sometime see you in the after life." He said, "Time is very short and will pass quickly like it did for him. Bridgetta Let's go eat I am very hungry now. Let's let great grandfather rest." "Ok! I'll visit with you later I love you! Great grandfather." "I Love you too!" I kissed him on his cheek and returned a hug.

We walked into the kitchen everyone was finished eating and the table was cleared. "Where is everyone?" I asked my grandmother and aunt they were finishing up the dishes. "They went to help for the ceremony tonight. We will have relative and friends and people from the village join in to-nights ceremony. Last night it was just our family. To night it will be different. "Will Jimmy and I still dance?" "Yes, Of course but we will have more dancers to join in you and Jimmy will be first then the other will follow. The dance will start earlier and the ceremony will end much later. Your father and grandfather are already explaining your brother and sisters what to expect. Jimmy hurry finish eating and go outside and explain to Bridgett to-nights Ceremony." We finished our breakfast and went outside.

"Come on, let's hurry to the ceremony grounds." He gabbed my hand and ran to the ceremony ground through the dusty road.

You could hear the bells and the beating of the drums as we approach the sacred ground. There were already people arriving to the event. The men were sitting in a large circle while the women were cooking a deer over the fire. "What's that smell the men are smoking?" I could smell as the breeze carried by me. "The men are smoking a peace pipe it has pie-o-ty. They smoke it to calm their spirits before the ceremony. There will be lots of people here with different levels of energy. This will help them prepare them self to connect to the spirits with out fear.

Tonight some will see a vision in their own way." "Jimmy, have you had vision?" "Of course! I started when I was five but I didn't need to smoke because I didn't know fear. I wasn't afraid of the spirits. Our great grandfather taught showed me how. So I grew up with out fear. Some of the men still have a little fear that why they smoke the pipe. Other wise fear will bring evil and a evil spirit will enter. Then we will have to chant away the evil spirit. That's why some of the customs have evil mask to keep away the evil spirits. Tonight will be a little stronger. See the Chief over there he is explaining to your brothers and sisters." "My brothers and sisters know of spirits. My mother and father taught us to chant. We have talk to spirits before, but not very often. But we know.

"Hey! Jimmy!" A voice cried from the crowd. "Hey! Jimmy!" I turned around to look for the voice. "Jimmy someone Is calling for you!" I grabbed him from the arm to shake for his attention. It was getting more crowded and the sound of the flute bells and the drum and people talking and visiting one another. Jimmy turned to look to see who it was. His eyes opened wide. "Hi, Running Bear. How are you doing? What's going on? This is my cousin.

Bridgett. Bridgett, let me introduce to you Running Bear. His name is Running Bear because when he was young he ran from a bear. He can out run any body. He's the fastest no one can beat him." "Come on Jimmy lets race?" "No, I don't want to be put to shame in front of Bridgett. You just want to show off. HA! HA!" Running Bear was very tall he was very good looking. My heart stopped I was stun I just stared lost for words. "Jimmy, why is she so white looking and you are so dark? Is she adopted cause she doesn't look Indian! She looks white!" I have never gave it much thought I've never really been approached like that I have always felt a little light but not white. I felt like an outcast. Jimmy laughed and I tried to laugh, "No She's number seven child and the color wore out when it was time for her to be born." HA! HA! HA! We all laughed. "That's a good one Jimmy!" "You got a beautiful cousin." I was impressed. He had long black hair passed his waist straight as a board. It was a hot summer day so he had blue jeans cutoffs I could see all the detail on his muscular body. I looked so strong looking down. He must have been a foot taller than me. Even taller than Jimmy. "Let's go get something to drink. I'm thirsty. What time are you going to put your costume on Jimmy?"

"It gets dark around 9:00 I guess 7:30 give me enough time before the ceremony. Bridgetta going to dance with me." "Wow! That's great! I would love to dance with her." He turned to me and winked his eye at me. My heart just couldn't stop beating so hard. I am going to stay close to you two. Watch out Jimmy future brother-in-law." He gave Jimmy a friendly shove. They both laughed. "Yea, right!"

"Shouldn't we start getting ready?" I asked them.

"Yea, Time sure does go by fast when your enjoying the moment." Running Bear said.

"Running Bear come over to my house and get dressed at my house!" "Let me ask my parents. I sure it will be alright." "Bye you guy's I'll see you at the ceremony." I rushed to the house to get dressed.

I Got to the house everybody was already taking a shower and getting ready for the ceremony. I didn't want to be in the crowded rooms. I just turned around and went outside to sit till it was less busy. I looked at the sun getting ready to set It was bright orange. The sky was turning from blue to purple. I could hear mother yelling to everyone. "Hurry up! Let's get great grandfather in the car." I turned to look Father and Sergio started out the door and headed to the car. They laid him gently in the back seat. Father came back to the house while Sergio waited in the car with great grandfather. "Bridgetta! Go inside and get dressed! Your still not ready? Hurry!"

"All right, Father! Is there room inside for me, it's so crowded in there. "Sure! I'll make room, come on. Everybody it's time to go. Get in the car or walk. Cause I am leaving now." Everybody rushed to the car. Father turned to me and smiled. "I told you I would make room!" He laughed. He knew they did like to walk in the dusty road. I didn't mind I Have always enjoyed walking even if it was a dusty road. The hot water was all used up I didn't mind to cool shower. It was so hot the cool shower felt good. I hurried and put my yellow costume on and head band with a yellow feather. It didn't take to long. I was ready in a jiffy. I rushed out the door and headed to the ceremony. I could hear the crowd as soon as I went out the door. I could see the light glaring high above the crowd. The sun had just set and the ceremony was just about to start. I searched through the crowded dancers There were a lot of adults to join the dance. There were hundreds of bells ringing. The flute was playing and everybody yelling so there was no point yelling for Jimmy. I just kept looking.

The drum started beating I knew it was time to start the dance. Then Jimmy grabbed my hand and Running Bear grabbed my other hand we entered the centered of the huge circle I was dancing with both of them I was surprised we were all together in step as everybody watched.

The dance was so quick. It ended so fast I wanted it to last forever. By the time I knew it Jimmy ended the dance with the feather in his mouth. Then to the outside of the circle we went to stand and watch the others dance. I turned to Jimmy. "Hey! You guys pulled a fast one on me. I didn't expect to dance with both of you. They looked at me and laughed. Running Bear put his arm around me pulled my head close to him and said. "It was my Idea. We thought you would enjoy the surprise. Did you?" "Yea, it was a great dance." "Yellow, looks great on you, it show up your tan beautiful." "Gee! Thanks!" I was so excited it seemed the crowd was gone for a moment and it was just Running bear and I. The time was going by fast. It must have been two hours before the end of the last dance. The stars were so bright and the moon was still lighting up the desert. Then the last three beats of the drum. Silence filled the crowd. Everyone sat and the chief stood from the crowd with one smug stick in each hand.

He began the sacred words as everybody listen not even a single word from a child. Complete silence. His words seem to move the spirits around. He began walking around the crowd with the smug sticks up and down and around. He went to the north, south, east, to west. Spirits began to move around everyone watched without fear. I Could see spirits from everywhere. The chief began talking to one spirit. You could see and hear the spirit, the sound were so different I couldn't understand if it was in the Indian language just to feel the spirit it was so peaceful and calm.

Jimmy turned to me and whispered. "He is telling the spirits that great grand father is very sick and will soon pass this life to the next life. We welcome the spirits to this sacred ground to prepare the time to travel on. The spirit knows of this and is prepared to welcome him to the universe of eternity life." There were other spirits around you could see them all over the sky. There were so many different spirits.

The spirit speaking to the chief began to swirl slowly then lifted up into the sky. Soon the others began to follow. A chant of good-by while the fire came to a very slow burn. The drum began to beat everybody stood then the end of the last drumbeat. Everyone looked up into the stars where to spirits vanished in to silence. The moon was shining so bright and the slow burning fire was enough light to see each other in the dark. Everyone stood up and began to visit each other.

"Bridgetta! My father called out. "We're heading home now it's late, it's time for you to go home!" "Hi Lujan, I'll walk Bridgetta home, if it's ok with you!" Jimmy asked. "Sure, I see you guys at the house. Bye!" My dad waved as he left. "Would it be alright if I come along?" Running Bear asked. "Sure, come on let's go." I said.

We headed back on the dusty road. The bells were ringing on Jimmy's and Running Bear's costumes it sounded to peaceful. I enjoyed the sound of the bells while we walked in the moonlight. "Wow! That was amazing. I love being an Indian. It's so exciting." I Wish I could stay on the reservation for the rest of my life." "Bridgetta! Will you come to the reservation where I live? I live on the other side of the mountain." Running Bear asked. "Which mountain?" I asked. "You know Rock with wings! You've heard that story haven't you?" Jimmy laughed. "Of course she has. Everybody knows that story!" I looked at Running Bear. Was that really a true story?" Running Bear looked at me sincere. "Your great grand father and my great grandfather were on the mountain when it lifted. I don't think they would make such a thing up." "Hey! Your right!" I said quickly. We reached the house. I got to the steps. "Well thanks for walking me home guys. I'll see you guys in the morning." "Alright! Bye!" I watched them leave on the dusty moon light road, until I couldn't hear the bells ringing. I turned and entered the house It was dark and everyone was already sleeping.

The next morning Javier shook me. "Bridgetta! Bridgetta! Wake up!" The sun wasn't quite up and the roaster didn't crow that morning. By the sound of Javier's Voice I sense there was something wrong. "What's the matter?" I knew for the moment that Great grandfather had left to the other side.

"Bridgetta! Great grandfather passed away an hour ago. Their getting him ready for tonight's ceremony, Everybody is awake and in the kitchen. I knew you would want me to wake you up. You must have been real tired. I had a hard time waking you up." "Yea, I am a little sore from all the dancing in the last few days." We weren't emotionally crying just sad but with peace of mind that his journey on this dimension was over. No more trials or pain. The universe was now his to travel.

It was quite and peaceful we were still all in our night clothes. The dogs began to howl and the coyotes where howling as well. I went outside and watched the sun rise.

Looking high up into the sky. My father came out and sat beside me. "Bridgett! That's a beautiful sunrise. It's so nice to watch the sunrise." "Father! Are we going to dance tonight for the ceremony? I don't feel like dancing tonight." "There will be one dancer the medicine man. He will be dressed and so will we but only he will dance then the ceremony. Let's go inside and eat some breakfast the get ready it's going to be a long day.

I finished breakfast and walked out the door to my favorite big rock. I sat on this rock and watched down the dusty road that leads to the rich aural grounds. I could see Running Bear coming up the trail. I watched him coming toward me in a slow motion while the sum stayed behind him forming a dark shadow until I looked up and there he was right up above me. If I moved in any direction my eyes would in the bright morning sun. Hotest day of the summer.

120 degrees in the shade, his voice spoke and my heart suddenly was beating so hard I could the blood pounding through my veins to the end of my fingers, and toes. I was in a state of shock. I couldn't move, I couldn't even bat my eyes. "Bridgetta, Bridgett! Bridgetta, are you all right?" His face was so close to my face. He reached with his finger tips so lightly I couldn't feel them. I knew he was touching me But I couldn't feel him.

I felt paralyzed by his energy. He picked up my hand and held it to his face. I could see he eyes now in the darkness. He turned me around Out of the sunlight. Is that better? Not knowing it was he not the sun. "Yes that's a lot better. I looked down at our hands and then up to see his face. He looked into my eyes and didn't have to say a word. We both knew why it was there by my side. Holding both hands tighter we both fighting our feelings to hold in each others arms. It wasn't the right moment we both knew. He lifted my arm up and squeezed my hands tighter.

He whispered looking in to my eyes. "That's how tight I want to hold you. I would never let you go if it were up to me. I have no control over this matter. But you know now, how I feel your pain with mine." I whispered back.

"I feel so weak. You drain all my energy. My heart beat is so strong. I could fly high If I could have a out of body experience with you?" Running Bear had tears running down his eyes. He took a deep breath with me and released very slowly at he same time and again. I could feel our hearts beat at the same time trying to slow the beat down together. We begin relaxing our thence muscles through the body. He releasing pressure through my finger. If I there were pain I didn't feel any pain at all. He gently rub my fingers with his fingers to bring back the circulations in my fingers. "It's so hard to let go!" I smiled. "I know!"

Can I come by and go with you and Jimmy. I'm ridding with Jimmy's family my family's car is full. My other cousin, Aunt and Uncle will ride along. Jimmy asked for me to go with them to the ceremony. I sure it would be fine. Because they have a pickup Lots of room. Running Bear looked around. "Let's go to the the feast.

Everyone eating together. Getting things ready for tonight. They had to gather all his clothing and his favorite bow and arrow and other things he liked that belong to him. "My father walked over to me. "Bridgetta, remember Rock with wings, the mountain? We will have the ceremony there is a sacred place on the mountain. Go home later, make sure you have plenty of time to be dressed and ready to welcome the spirits."

"Alright, father!" We walked around the quite feast for a while.
Time was silence. There wasn't much conversation being passed around. "I'm going home to get dressed and beat everyone to the shower. I'll be ready early and be on the mountain early. Jimmy do you think your parents would like to arrive early on the mountain top?" Jimmy questioned. "I'll ask!" He went not to far away. Running Bear and I waited in silence, then his short return. "They said that's a good Idea. They are leaving now to get ready. Let's go get ready."

I was ready in the shortest time. I waited outside for them to show up. They let my parents know before they left the feast. I saw the dust of cloud coming at a distance, it was them. We started diving toward the mountain. Time went by so fast. We got to beginning of the mountain and stopped. "We have to walk the rest of the way up the mountain. There were rocks placed on the trail for steps that took us up the mountain. 45 minuets we arrived at the sacred rock. At the bottom of a large cliff, high up the mountain. The mountain is larger when viewing from the edge of the rock. I looked around. My Aunt Betty grabbed a bush to dust away the dirt that had been collected over the years. I grabbed another bush and started dusting with her. We cleaned up around and began place dried Sage bushes and other bushes I didn't know the name the plants that were gathered and placed on the rock. Later my mom and dad arrived with his belongings and placed them on the outside of the circle.

The sun was setting down on the basin it was time for the wrapped body arrive. We could hear the chant coming at a distance and could see the glare of the fire torches carried in the dark a trail from the bottom the rock.

The body was the last in the trail of torches. He was placed in the center of the large group of bushes. We all were in a spiral circle at a distance of the bushes. The chief raised the smug sticks up toward the stars, saying the sacred words. The dance of the medicine man began. The medicine man then lifted the smug sticks up and around the circle of fire. The spirits began falling around us in a spiral motion one by one It reminded me of falling stars falling around us so fast. It felt like we were in a dome, a shield. After the spirits fell, you could see Angels appear in the lighted dome. Angels you don't see in books they are so different. I looked around as they appeared. Something said to look up above me, as I did it was my guardian above me. They were all close above us all. The fire burning the body was intense. It became brighter, high above the sky. The Chief then spoke into the fire welcome the spirit of my great grand father lifted in the fire. There was another spirit in the fire. He came to guide him in the light. This was our way of saying good by to see he made it to the other side high up into universe, eternity. The fire was so bright you could see the spirit ready to leave. The spirit in the fire swished up in to the sky and then my great father swished up into the sky. One after another swished up so fast that in seconds the spirits were gone. The fire went out leaving the ashes burning in the rock. Then the wind blew hard blowing the ashes over the mountain. It was almost time for the sun to rise. We spiraled our way to the trail that headed down the to the dusty road making our way back to the village.

978-0-595-84185-1
0-595-84185-6

Printed in the United States
54276LVS00001B/34-72